The 90s Club

& the Mystery of the Brassbound Trunk

Eileen Haavik McIntire

Amanita Books
Imprint of Summit Crossroads Press
Columbia, Maryland USA

ISBN: 978-1-7368214-6-6

Library of Congress Control Number: 2025903944

Cover design by Earthly Charms, earthlycharms.com

Considering door prizes for your reunion or senior event? Any book in the 90s Club series can be ordered in bulk quantities of 10 or more at the publisher's discounted price. Contact the publisher at amanitabooks@aol.com.

Website: SecretPanels.net.

Published by Amanita Books, an imprint of Summit Crossroads Press, and printed in the United States of America. Contact Amanita Books by email at amanitabooks@aol.com.

Dedicated to
Eugenia (Gene) Somers, age 96,
who went snorkeling when
they told her she shouldn't,
and
Inge Hyder, age 94,
who jumped out of a plane on
her 80th and 90th birthdays.
ABLE, ALERT, AND ACTIVE

Books by Eileen Haavik McIntire

The 90s Club cozy mysteries
The 90s Club & the Hidden Staircase
The 90s Club & the Whispering Statue
The 90s Club & the Secret of the Old Clock
The 90s Club & the Mystery at Lilac Inn
The 90s Club & the Clue in the Old Album
*The 90s Club & the Mystery of
the Brass-Bound Trunk*

Historical Mysteries
Shadow of the Rock
In Rembrandt's Shadow (Sequel)

Suspense
The Two-Sided Set-Up
The House on Hatemonger Hill

Acknowledgements

Thank you to the stalwart fans of the 90s Club series and to all those who envision the "elderly" as able, alert, and active.

When I first started writing this series, my critique group told me I should make my characters feeble, odd, deaf, and walker- or wheelchair-bound. Some readers echoed their comments. My critique group also saw Whisperwood as an "old folks' home" or nursing home. When filet mignon was on the menu in my book, one person said, "no way."

Times have changed, I'm happy to say. Now, readers are likely to tell me about "Uncle Harry" who is 95 and hikes the Appalachian Trail or "Aunt Susie" who wins the annual canoe race in her community. Old doesn't have to mean crippled, but our culture often insists that it be so.

I also think people are more aware now of upscale retirement places like Whisperwood that are definitely not "nursing homes." They offer a smorgasbord of activities, menu items that do include filet mignon, and pleasant apartments.

In this series, I hope to be one of many changing

the paradigm of what it means to be elderly.

Thank you to critique group members Flo McCahon, who writes the Faraday cozy mystery series as Millie Mack, and Janis Wilson, author of *Goulston Street: The Quest for Jack the Ripper.*

Thanks also to beta readers Frances Altman, Stephen M. Berberich, Reggie Greenberg, Amy Gunarich, Maureen Klovers, and Ken Stepanuk.

During my college years, I worked at Tilghman Company, a fine jewelry store in Annapolis, MD. My boss was Tom Tilghman, Jr., who was kind, supportive, and enthusiastic. He taught me about charting and weighing diamonds, used my artistic talents in jewelry design, and loaned me his textbooks from the Gemological Institute of America. In this book, I updated a bit of what I learned from him. Thank you, Tom Tilghman.

Most of all, I thank my husband, Roger McIntire, for providing love and support.

I strive to be accurate, but I can make mistakes. Any errors are entirely my doing.

Eileen Haavik McIntire

Chapter 1

Nancy ran a hand through her curly white hair and relaxed, grateful to be alive. She had almost died in their last adventure. Now things were back to normal. She sat at her table in the lobby of Whisperwood Retirement Village, laptop open, ready to inform and protect residents besieged by the numerous scams and frauds targeting them.

In truth, she was feeling a bit bored.

Whisperwood was a six-story, U-shaped building set on top of a flattened mountaintop in central West Virginia. A long road wound its way from the nearest small town through the woods and up the mountain to reach the Whisperwood gates. Even though Whisperwood offered a wide range of activities for its residents, Nancy sometimes missed the bright lights, theaters, and restaurants available in a large city.

She watched a scruffy young man wearing a white tee shirt, jeans, and leather workboots stride through the entrance. A warm breeze redolent with the fragrance of late-spring flowers and freshly mown grass followed him in. He hesitated inside the door and looked around, spotted Nancy, and headed for her.

"How may I help you?" she asked pleasantly.

"I need to see the manager of this place," the man said. "The one in charge."

"That would be Harry Doyle, Whisperwood administrator. I believe he is in his office." She nodded toward the other side of the lobby where a glass door engraved with the words "Executive Suite" opened into a large space with several small offices.

The reception desk, actually a high counter with a sign-in register for guests, stood in front of the glass door. A young woman leaned on the counter, coffee cup in hand.

"Ask the receptionist," Nancy said.

"Okay. Thanks."

The man walked to the counter. Just then, Harry opened the door to one of the offices in the suite and walked out with a short, thin, middle-aged man and a tall, attractive African-American woman in a powder blue suit.

"Nancy," Harry exclaimed, leading his two companions over to her table, "just the person I want to see. Let me introduce our new staff, Gene Reynolds, finance director, and Violet Velois, program director."

"Actually, my title is Life Enrichment Director," Violet said, glancing at Harry. "I'll be handling entertainment and other programs for the residents."

"Wonderful!" Nancy exclaimed, standing. "Welcome. I am pleased to meet you both." And how. Their last finance director was in jail, and the auditor was still cleaning up the mess she had made.

They shook hands. Both new hires were beaming.

"A pleasure," Gene Reynolds said. "My wife and kids are looking forward to living the rural life." He grinned. "My daughter wants a horse."

"I am thrilled at this opportunity," said Violet. I hope to come up with exciting programs for you." Her eyes were expressive and brown and her voice had the sultry tones of a blues singer.

At this point, the receptionist intervened and introduced the man standing at the counter. "This is Mr. Alex Elmo," she said. "Here to see Mr. Doyle."

Harry smiled at the visitor and invited him into his office.

"Thought we'd take a walk around," Violet said. "Nice to meet you." Gene and Violet excused themselves and wandered down the hall.

Nancy waved them on as her friend Louise popped out of the elevator and headed toward her table. Louise wore her usual khaki pants and a blue polo shirt along with a button advocating one cause or another. This one read, "Vaccinations Save Lives! Remember Polio?"

"You're a sitting duck for anyone who walks in the door," Louise said. "You trying to take her job?" She nodded at the receptionist.

Nancy laughed. "I get enough business. You wouldn't believe how many residents come to me worried they've been scammed or made some mistake on their computer."

"I believe it," snorted Louise. "We're all targets for scammers worldwide. You do good work here."

"I rely on the 90s Club," said Nancy, referring to their small group of 90-year-olds, all able, alert, and active. They had gained respect and admiration as crime solvers among the residents of Whisperwood.

The office door opened and Alex Elmo stepped out of the executive suite holding a slip of paper in his hand. He walked briskly to the exit as Harry watched him and then ambled over to Nancy and Louise, shaking his head.

"Here's a new wrinkle," Harry said, nodding at the departing young man. "Remember Glinda Spencer? Resident who died a year ago?" *

"She was murdered," said Nancy, thinking of Glinda's vividly pink apartment and the horror of facing her two staring stuffed cats. "Hard to forget." Very few people besides Nancy knew that Glinda had also been a petty thief and a blackmailer, extorting small sums each month from her victims.

"Glinda was trouble when she was alive," said Louise, "and now she's still trouble after being dead for a year." Louise's lip curled. "And she deliberately misspelled her name, so she could turn the dot over the "i" into a star. Always looking for attention."

"That man wants her steamer trunk," Harry said. "I didn't even know she had one. What is it, anyway?"

"It's like a footlocker," put in Louise.

"Years ago, they used to pack them for travel, but they were heavy and awkward," said Nancy. "I saw Glinda's. It was wooden with brass fittings, about three feet by almost two feet and maybe two feet high. I helped her move it once. It was too large for her apartment."

"Do you know what happened to it?" Harry asked.

"Didn't one of her sons take it?" Nancy said.

*See *The 90s Club & the Hidden Staircase.*

Glinda had two sons, named after movie stars, Cary and Clark. Nancy remembered watching Cary and his wife carry boxes out of Glinda's apartment. They could have loaded the trunk with her stuff and taken it home or put it in the dumpster. Her other son Clark was an alcoholic and immersed in his problems.

Harry shrugged and rapped on the receptionist's counter. "Glinda's sister Barbara Elmo lives here with her husband Don. Alex says he's their grandson. He wanted their apartment number, so I called them for permission. They seemed surprised but glad to see him. He wanted Cary's phone number, too."

"They can probably tell him what it is," Louise said.

Harry shrugged and walked back to his office, muttering to himself.

Nancy tapped her lips thoughtfully. "I do remember seeing that trunk after she died, but I don't know what happened to it."

"Forget it, Nancy," said Louise. "It'll turn up."

Nancy closed her laptop and went back to her apartment at noon. She couldn't help wondering what happened to Glinda's steamer trunk and why a young man like Alex was searching for it.

As she entered the apartment, her fiancé Fitz Connelly looked up from the book he was reading. "How did it go?"

"Not many takers this morning, but a man named Alex Elmo walked in asking about Glinda's steamer trunk. Claims he's her great-nephew. Remember Glinda?"

Fitz shuddered. "Who could forget her? 'The

Singing Canary.' The so-called star who disrupted your Spanish class."

"And you didn't even see her stuffed cats." Nancy kissed Fitz on his forehead. "Alex wants her old brassbound trunk."

"Odd," said Fitz. "Nobody uses those anymore."

"Harry also introduced me to two new staff members—a finance director and a program director."

Fitz shook his head. "I hope he checked their references carefully this time. We need a competent and honest finance director." Fitz returned to reading his book.

Memories rushed through Nancy's mind. She had almost lost Fitz in the 90s Club's last case.* She never wanted to go through that again.

She pulled out sandwich fixings for lunch but couldn't stop wondering about the trunk. She made a quick decision and picked up her address book. She found Cary's phone number and called on her landline. His wife Teresa answered.

"I'm here at Whisperwood," said Nancy. "I knew Cary's mother Glinda and helped you move a few boxes out of her apartment."

"Oh yes. And you caught her killer, too," said Teresa. "We are thankful for that."

"It wasn't me," demurred Nancy. "The 90s Club and my cat Malone were the heroes."

"We're grateful to all of you," Teresa said, dispensing with the nonsense, "but how can I help you?"

"Glinda had a steamer trunk..." Nancy began.

Teresa laughed. "That battered old thing? Heavy, awkward, and useless, but Glinda had to have it. You're

*See *The 90s Club & the Clue in the Old Album.*

the second person today who has called us about it."

"And I'll bet the first was Alex Elmo, right?" said Nancy. "He said Glinda was his great-aunt. He came to Whisperwood looking for it and the administrator, Harry Doyle, gave him your phone number. Harry doesn't know anything about it, but I started wondering what happened to it."

"Alex is Barbara Elmo's grandson. He thinks he has some kind of right to that trunk, but like I told him, we don't have any idea where it is," said Teresa. "It's not here, but I vaguely remember coming across it when we cleaned out her apartment. I told him to ask his grandmother, Barbara. She lives there at Whisperwood. Maybe she knows something."

"Okay, thanks," Nancy said and called Barbara, but she also claimed to know nothing about the trunk. Nancy could think of no one else to ask.

Glinda had been proud of that trunk. It meant something to her, so she wouldn't have sold it or given it away. But what had happened to it?

When Glinda had asked Nancy to help her move the trunk, she had taken out of it a historic Russian boundary plate found in Alaska. "This is one of those plates," Glinda had told her, "the Russians planted around Alaska to mark their territory. Nineteenth century, I think."

"How did you get it?" Nancy had asked in awe. "It belongs in a museum."

"Never mind," Glinda had said. Then she had displayed the plate on the shelf in the hall and, as Nancy predicted, someone had stolen it.

The trunk was empty when Nancy had last seen

it. Why did Alex want it and why did he wait a year to come looking for it?

Meet the New Staff

Welcome new staff members Gene Reynolds, Finance Director, and Violet Velois, Life Enrichment Director.

Gene hails from Wichita, Kansas, has a B.A. degree in Finance from West Virginia University, and is certified as a CPA. Among his proud accomplishments is hiking the Appalachian Trail twice. He also enjoys rock climbing and other outdoor activities. He and his wife and two kids are looking forward to living in the country.

Violet Velois is an entertainer herself and has many contacts in the world of theater and media. She looks forward to scheduling fine lectures and performances for you.

The Whisperwood Breeze,
Newsletter of Whisperwood
Retirement Village

Chapter 2

Fitz had emailed Harry Doyle for a copy of Gene Reynolds' resumé, studied it, and asked Nancy to do an Internet search on him. What Nancy found agreed with the resumé and didn't include even a hint of criminal activity, so Fitz had gone out to meet the new finance director.

Nancy was trying to read a book as she relaxed before dinner, but her obnoxious cat Malone prowled restlessly in the foyer, occasionally scratching at the door. Then she heard a faint knock. As she walked to the door, she heard mewing from the other side and Malone growled and sniffed at the crack under the door. Nancy opened the door cautiously, stepped out, and closed it behind her, leaving Malone inside complaining in his most displeased voice.

A tall, slim woman in her sixties stood in the hall. "I'm Caroline Richards," the new neighbor said. "I just moved here from Baltimore." She held a fidgeting black "tuxedo" kitten in her arms and was dressed casually in jeans and a ruffled white shirt, but she had piled on the face powder, red lipstick, and dark pencil brows. Her hair was brown and curly. "Sorry to disturb you, but my kitten Cleo ran out of my apartment and over to your door. She's normally a nice kitty, but now she hisses, spits, and claws at me when I try to pick her up. I don't know what to do."

"That's odd, isn't it?" Nancy introduced herself. "My cat Malone has been prowling by the door for two days. He is neutered, though." Malone wanted to meet their new cat neighbor. The revelation astounded her. But did he want to play or fight? Could he possibly be lonely?

Caroline nodded. "That's when we moved in."

Inside the apartment, Malone quieted down as he heard their voices in the hall, but the kitten hissed, jumped out of Caroline's arms, and ran to the door. She sniffed at the crack.

"Your kitty must sense a new cat in the neighborhood," said Caroline. The kitten purred and Malone scratched even more furiously behind the closed door. "Maybe Malone and Cleo could become friends."

Nancy almost smiled. Caroline was new here and had never met Malone or heard the stories about him. That's why she could make such an audacious suggestion. Nancy hoped this woman would still be smiling after she met Malone.

Fawn-colored with the temperament of a bobcat, Malone was not everyone's kitty, but he had caught two vicious killers at Whisperwood. What would he do with Cleo? Nancy shuddered at the thought. "Malone can be a bit ... prickly," she said, "but they want to meet each other."

"Cleo is such a gentle kitten most times, but I heard the stories about your cat even before I moved here," Caroline said. "He has quite a personality, but a little female kitty might tame him. We could let them get together and see what happens."

"Okay," Nancy said dubiously. "Our two cats seem to be sniffing at each other through the crack." She opened the door slowly.

Cleo ran past Nancy into the foyer and stopped to stare at Malone. Malone stared back. Then they each tentatively moved forward to sniff the other. Their people watched, spellbound.

He's not going to hurt her, is he?" Caroline said.

Malone and Cleo rubbed each other's heads.

"I don't know," said Nancy.

"I'm afraid to do anything," whispered Caroline.

Nancy nodded. "Me, too."

They watched the kitty courtship a while longer, then Nancy went to her kitchen to search for the tastiest cat treat she could find. Tuna.

Malone loved tuna. Nancy divided it, giving half to Malone and enticing Cleo to move away before giving the other half to Caroline. Caroline used it to lure Cleo into the hall and gave it to her there. Nancy followed, closing the door behind her. Cleo finished the tuna, and Caroline picked her up.

"Thank you," she said, nuzzling Cleo.

"They seem to like each other," said Nancy. "Malone could use a friend. We'll talk about this later," said Nancy. "Maybe they can have play dates."

She returned to her apartment, closed the door, and stroked Malone on the head and back. For once he accepted the loving gesture. She marveled at this new dimension to Malone. He had a girlfriend!

Later, she strode down the hall to join Fitz, Louise, and their friend George Burroughs for dinner in Whisperwood's dining room. The four of them were the 90s Club. Residents called them the "Rescuers of Whisperwood," although most people knew Malone was the true hero in bringing down the villains who preyed on the residents. Nobody messed with Malone.

The dining room had been recently redecorated. The aqua and peach color scheme had given way to forest green and white with mint green napkins in place on white tablecloths.

George decorated his short, pudgy body with a lemon-colored shirt, neon pink tie, and sky-blue slacks. As he explained, he loved color. He caught everyone's eye as he walked to the 90s Club's favorite table, number fifty-six near the wall and behind a wide pillar to ensure privacy. Their high school server, too young to handle alcohol, filled the water glasses and left to summon the manager to get their wine orders.

Nancy quickly perused the menu and settled on her new favorite, broiled trout in lemon sauce with capers. The server took their orders and disappeared as the manager arrived with a chilled bottle of *Pinot Grigio.*

"So what's on the agenda tonight?" asked Louise in her gravelly voice. This time, the button pinned to her polo shirt said, "Climate Change is Real."

"Harry has made two new hires," said Nancy. "Did you read the notice in the newsletter?"

"I'm glad they found someone to book outside entertainment for us," said Louise, "but they dreamed up a fancy new title for her: Life Enrichment Director."

"I'm looking forward to interesting lectures and entertainment beyond the local bluegrass band," said Fitz. "They're all right, but I'd like more variety."

"Me, too," agreed George.

"Gene Reynolds has hiked the trail and has a wife and kids," said Nancy. "The newsletter didn't say much about Violet Velois."

"She probably gets tired of people shmoozing her," said George. "We'll have to wait and see."

"On another subject, Glinda's steamer trunk," said Nancy. "No one seems to know where it is."

Louise laughed and clapped her hands. "I knew you'd call her son. Cary, wasn't it? He didn't know anything?" She flicked the long braid that ran down her back.

"No. Harry doesn't either, and Cary's brother Clark barely showed his face here, so I'm sure he doesn't have it." Nancy sipped her wine.

Fitz twirled his wine glass. "Do you suppose it was another item stolen by the previous administration?"

"Maybe it was taken to the thrift shop for sale," suggested Louise.

Nancy nodded. "They're open tomorrow. I'll drop by."

"Who was asking about it?" asked George. "Why would anyone be interested?"

"Glinda's great-nephew Alex walked in today while I was in the lobby and talked to Harry," said Nancy. "Harry gave him Cary's phone number and Alex called him. I helped Glinda with it once. It was old, battered, and held together with brass strips. I can't imagine it was worth much in that condition."

"It's the kind of thing people would turn into coffee tables or storage chests for blankets nowadays," said Louise.

George arched an eyebrow. "Do you really believe a young man would want a steamer trunk for his coffee table? I doubt that unless it has money in it."

The server placed their meals before them, and George eyed the steak he had ordered.

"Alex is Barbara and Don Elmo's grandson, so maybe he has fond memories of it. After all, Glinda was his great aunt." Nancy sat back and took another sip of wine. Alex had been respectful enough when he asked, no, *demanded* to see Harry Doyle, but he had also acted entitled. Entitled to see Doyle or to acquire the trunk?

Later, as Fitz and Nancy walked hand in hand back to their apartment, they heard a fierce meow followed by the loud scratching sound of claws on wood.

"Malone!" Nancy looked at Fitz, and they both ran to the door and opened it cautiously.

Their overlarge cat Malone tried to dart through the crack between their legs and out into the hall, but Fitz and Nancy blocked him as they entered and closed the door quickly. "What's going on with him?" Fitz asked.

Nancy shook her head. "He wants to see his girlfriend next door." She examined the inside of the door where Malone's claws had left long cracks in the paint. He glared at them and growled, then sat and stared at the door as the humans walked past him into the living room.

***

The Second Time Around Treasure Thrift Shop in the basement opened at ten a.m. on Wednesdays. Caroline Richards walked out of her apartment at the same time as Nancy. "Where are you off to?" asked Caroline.

"Have you been to the thrift shop yet?" Nancy asked. "Great place to donate items you no longer need and find ones you're missing."

"Wonderful," said Caroline. "Mind if I tag along?"

Nancy could hardly refuse her, so Nancy, Louise, and Caroline were waiting when Paige Lincoln arrived a few minutes late to open the door.

"Sorry," she muttered, fumbling with the keys in embarrassment. "Usually get here early but got a phone call from my son."

"That's all right," assured Nancy. "We're not in a rush."

Paige smiled. "That's good. We've got a lot of useful treasures here; some of them are almost new. You need to take your time to browse."

"My best spatula broke," Louise said, wandering to the kitchen utensils area.

"I'm hoping you can help me solve a little mystery," said Nancy while Caroline browsed nearby. Paige loved reading mysteries and often urged Nancy to explain again how she solved the Whisperwood murders.

"Mystery. This sounds good. Tell me more," said Paige.

"Do you remember Glinda Spencer?"

She shuddered. "Her son brought her stuffed dead

cats here for me to sell. Can you imagine? I told him to give them a decent burial."

"That was the right thing to do." But Nancy had seen the black plastic bag Cary used to deposit them in the trash bin. "Glinda had a steamer trunk, too. It was wooden with brass trim. Did anything like that come through the thrift shop?"

"Oh, my. No. I would have remembered. They did bring down a fake Tiffany lamp, though. At least, I think it was a fake. Can't imagine she'd have a real one." She laughed and winked at Nancy.

Nancy remembered that lamp. It was beautiful, and she didn't think it was a fake.

"What happens to items that don't sell?" asked Nancy.

"I pack them up and call an antique dealer down the road who buys the stuff by the boxload. We don't get much for it, but at least it's out of here." She paused to straighten a line of bric-a-brac. "Anyway, nobody uses a steamer trunk nowadays. We've got those light suitcases with wheels. Much easier and you don't need a crew of people to carry it."

Nancy agreed and spent a few minutes browsing, but the last thing she wanted was more stuff. She recognized several items that had been treasures of residents, now gone, whose sons or daughters wasted no time unloading unwanted keepsakes onto the thrift shop.

Caroline had been examining the large collection of donated clothes.

Paige walked over to her. "Do you know anything about clothes?"

"A bit," Caroline admitted. "Worked with theater wardrobes. You know, costumes. Some of these are classics by well-known designers. They're worth a lot more than you're charging."

Paige fluttered her hands. "I don't know anything about clothes or designers, but if you do, I could sure use your help."

"I'll be glad to, and I can start right now," Caroline said and began leafing through the racks.

"Ready to go?" Nancy asked. The place made her sad with its mementos and remnants of lives now gone. She never stayed long.

"I'm helping Paige," said Caroline. "You go on."

Louise paid for her purchases and joined Nancy in wandering down the hall toward the elevator. Nancy stopped to stare at the deserted end of the basement hall.

Only a year ago, that end wall had hidden a secret door into the labyrinth of mining tunnels under Whisperwood. A "Danger" sign on the wall had warned of electrical equipment and kept inquisitive residents away from the area, but the tunnels had been used for criminal activities and once the crooks were caught, the tunnels had been blocked and filled in. The sign remained, but now the wall was simply that. A plain, white wall.

Nancy took a closer look. Or was it?

Thrift Shop Bonanza!
Designer dresses galore! Beautiful decorator items! Kitchen gear and much more! The Second Time Around Trea-

sure Thrift Shop in the basement is open Wednesday mornings from ten a.m. until noon. We are overstocked with designer dresses in smaller sizes, given to us by residents who have been enjoying our good meals too much. Ha ha! Small furniture items are also in good supply, so if you need a lamp, chair, or decorative wall hanging, see us first!

The Whisperwood Breeze,
Newsletter of the Whisperwood
Retirement Village

Chapter 3

Nancy sat in the shade of the portico, enjoying the summer breezes and watching Alex walking through the parking lot toward her. He wore brown shorts with a white tee shirt and carried a backpack.

As he approached, Nancy called out to him. "Hello, I'm Nancy Dickinson. I understand you're Barbara Elmo's grandson and Glinda Spencer was your great-aunt."

He stopped and stared at her with calculation in his eyes. "That's right," he said. "I was very close with Aunt Glinda. She came from Alaska. We spent a lot of time together there."

"I'm sorry for your loss," Nancy said.

"Thank you." He sat on the bench next to Nancy. "I'm going to stay here for a few days in one of the hotel rooms they have for relatives. Aunt Glinda was in show business, you know. People called her 'The Singing Canary.'"

"She mentioned that," Nancy said, keeping a straight face. Glinda had been one of the most obnoxious people she'd ever known. She had told everyone she was called 'The Singing Canary,' trite as it was.

"Did anything special bring you down to our wild and wonderful West Virginia?" Nancy asked. *Why did he want an old, battered, outmoded steamer trunk?*

"The Anchorage newspaper ran an article about her a couple of weeks ago. I heard Aunt Glinda had died, but I couldn't make it to the memorial service. I was real sorry about that. This was the soonest I could come for a visit." He paused, staring down at his hands. "Then I heard Cary and Clark had taken over her apartment and pretty much thrown out everything she owned. That made me mad. I'm a taxidermist and those cats were state of the art, they were. No call to throw them away like trash."

"I see," Nancy said, hoping her face didn't reveal her revulsion.

"And I gave her a beautiful antique steamer trunk, and I hear that's missing, too." Anger crept into his voice. "Cary claims he knows nothing about it. I believe him about that. He and that wife of his have no appreciation for old things unless they're in perfect condition. They even gave away the Tiffany lamp! And what happened to the Russian boundary plaque? That ought to be in a museum."

"The man who killed her was also a thief. He stole many valuable items from the residents here," Nancy said, omitting the fact that Glinda had picked up trinkets and sentimental items off the residents' display shelves and hidden them in her apartment.

"What happened to the things he stole?" asked Alex.

"They were returned to the residents or their relatives. A few went to the gift shop."

"Except no one knows where the steamer trunk is. I want that trunk."

"I know you talked to Harry Doyle, the administrator, about it," said Nancy. "He asked me to look into its disappearance. I checked with Whisperwood's thrift shop, but they know nothing about it. I'll put a note in *The Whisperwood Breeze*, our newsletter, asking for information on its whereabouts."

"Good," said Alex. "I'd appreciate anything you can do." He rose. "Now I've got to check in with my grandparents. I went into town for dinner last night. The food here any good?"

"Excellent," said Nancy and watched Alex stride through the front door of Whisperwood.

Later, she closed her book, picked up her tote bag, and walked to the building entrance. A tall, stringy man beat her to the door and pulled it open for her. A whiff of alcohol floated by. He wore a blue polo shirt with jeans and fanned himself with his broad-brimmed hat despite the air-conditioned chill that greeted them in the lobby. He walked to the reception desk and asked for the person in charge. Nancy had never seen him before. She watched him disappear into Harry Doyle's office and then strolled to the reception desk to pump the receptionist, a young woman named Ashley.

"New resident here?" Nancy asked.

Ashley shook her head. "Wanted to talk to Mr. Doyle. That's all I know."

In a few minutes, Harry opened his office door and bowed the stranger out, then he saw Nancy.

"Wait a minute, sir," he said. "Nancy, this is Sterling Cooper. He says he is Glinda Spencer's ex-husband and is inquiring about her belongings, especially the steamer trunk. Were you able to find out where it might be?"

Nancy noted Harry's emphasis on the word "says" and replied cautiously. "Hello, Mr. Cooper, I'm sorry for your loss."

Sterling Cooper peered at Nancy out of a weathered face, tanned and wrinkled. "Yes, I was out at my cabin in Alaska, workin' the tourists. Didn't hear about her passing till a couple of weeks ago. I used to manage her act. They called her 'The Singing Canary,' you know."

Nancy winced. "She told us about that," she said. "We've had other inquiries about her steamer trunk, but I haven't been able to locate it. I'm afraid it might have been disposed of after she died."

Sterling's face turned red. "What do you mean, disposed of? What other inquiries? That trunk belongs to me. I loaned it to her, and she promised to give it back to me. It belongs to my family."

"I'm sorry..." Nancy began, but Sterling interrupted her.

"Did you ask that sister of hers? Barbara?" he asked. "Or Barbara's deadbeat husband? Glinda's sons, Cary and Clark?"

"I've talked to everyone I could think of, but no one knows where it is."

Sterling put his hands on his hips and glared at Nancy. "I can see I'll have to investigate this myself." He turned to Harry. "Where does Glinda's sister live?"

Harry stepped back as if he expected a punch. "I can't give out that information, sir."

"What?" Sterling screeched. "Why not? I'm her brother-in-law. That was."

"If you give me a phone number, I'll ask her to call you."

Harry glanced at Nancy as if for support.

"That's the rule here," she added, glad that Harry showed such good sense. He hadn't always done so. Sterling looked angry and out of control. She'd hate to have him show up at her door unannounced.

"I'm staying at the motel down the road. I don't have a cell phone. Tell her to leave a message there." He jammed his hat on his head and turned to leave. "I'll be back, don't you worry."

Nancy, Harry, and Ashley watched him leave.

"Didn't the other man, Alex Elmo, Glinda's nephew, say he'd given the trunk to Glinda?" Nancy asked.

"The plot thickens," said Harry and returned to his office, closing the door behind him.

Lost Steamer Trunk

Relatives of former resident Glinda Spencer are searching for a steamer trunk that was in Glinda's possession at the time of her passing. It was an old-fashioned wooden trunk with brass fittings, probably manufactured in the 1930s. If you have seen it or know where it is, please contact Ashley at the Reception Counter.

The Whisperwood Breeze,
Newsletter of Whisperwood
Retirement Village

Chapter 4

Dinner that evening was spent brainstorming ideas about why Glinda's ex-husband and her great-nephew both claimed her brassbound trunk.

"Could it be an antique worth thousands?" asked Louise.

Nancy shook her head. "I looked it up on several antique auction sites. To sell for more than a hundred bucks, it would have to be in excellent condition, well cared for, and probably a real antique more than a hundred years old. Glinda's trunk was battered, in poor condition, and maybe dated from the 1930s."

"Wouldn't be worth the trip to come here and get it," said George.

"What was inside it?" asked Louise.

"Nothing, as far as we know," Nancy said, "but the thrift shop hasn't seen it, and no one else seems to know anything about it."

George shrugged. "Probably in the landfill," he grumbled.

Nancy went on to tell George and Louise about Malone's girlfriend Cleo. "She's a kitten and our new neighbor doesn't know how to handle her."

"Maybe she'll tame Malone," said Louise, "which may not be a good thing. His aggressive, wild nature has saved your life twice."

Nancy nodded. "We'll have to wait and see what happens. Cleo's owner, Caroline Richards, moved in only a couple of days ago."

As they walked out to the hall after dinner, two women accosted them.

"People were telling us about you all during dinner," gushed one, wearing a brown pantsuit and athletic shoes. "I'm Vicki Townsend and this is my sister Bella Shore. We just moved here."

"Welcome," said Nancy and introduced herself and Fitz, who nodded a greeting. George mumbled his name and Louise waved. Nancy saw that the role of host was up to her. "We enjoy living here, and I'm sure you will, too," she added with a smile.

"We heard you are Whisperwood's detectives," Bella said. "You must tell us all about it." With her pink complexion and rosy cheeks, she looked like an elderly kewpie doll. She was wearing a flowery and frilly dress with strappy high heels. Her gaze wandered to the passersby leaving the dining room.

Nancy glanced at the other 90s Club members.

Louise stepped in. "We try to help when we see something going wrong," she said.

Bella tittered. "I'm sure it's more than that from what the others said."

George took the moment to excuse himself and headed down the hall.

Bella watched him with a slight smile on her face. "He's quite a handsome man," she said to Louise with a lascivious wink.

Louise choked. Pudgy, bald George? Handsome? Too much. Louise waved goodbye. "Got to go. See you tomorrow," she said.

Nancy and Fitz also took their leave, and Nancy wondered how Louise would take Bella's obvious interest in George. Louise and George were close friends. How close?

They walked into the apartment. Malone sat in the foyer, licking his paws and looking smug. "Something is off here," said Fitz, "but I don't know what it is."

"Malone is usually asleep on the couch when we return from dinner." Nancy glanced around the room. "I feel it, too."

Fitz shrugged. "I don't see anything wrong or out of place."

Nancy agreed. "Probably our imaginations."

***

The next morning, Nancy met Louise by the residents' community garden. Louise wore her usual jeans and polo shirt garb with a button pinned on her shirt that said, "Support Your Local Humane Society." Nancy wore white Bermuda shorts with a white T-shirt and sneakers. She was meeting Fitz later at the tennis court.

"We are starting the trail here," said Louise, explaining her latest project, a hiking path from Whisperwood grounds to what would soon be a county park behind the buildings. Thanks to an anti-quarry campaign waged by Whisperwood residents, the application to strip mine that area had been rejected.

"Perfect," said Nancy. "The gardens draw a lot of

residents who'll be able to extend their walk into the park."

Louise surveyed the grounds with satisfaction. "And the path will be paved on Whisperwood land for those in wheelchairs. On parkland, it will be mulched."

"Sounds good," said Nancy, nodding. She began walking along the designated pathway, not yet paved but marked by small green flags. As they passed one of the storage sheds behind the garden, she noticed a man sitting against the building. "Is that man all right?" she asked. "He's not moving."

"We'd better check," Louise answered, walking toward him. "The weather is heating up; maybe he had a heat stroke."

"That's Alex Elmo," Nancy said as they approached. His backpack lay on the ground next to him.

"Does he work here?" asked Louise. "He's too young to be a resident."

"He's a great nephew of Glinda Spencer. You know, The Singing Canary," Nancy said.

"How could I forget her?" Louise muttered as they approached. "Something's wrong. That looks like blood on his shirt."

Blood had spurted from the hole in the man's chest and spread on his shirt. "He's not breathing either." Nancy pulled out her cell phone and called 911. Then she checked her watch. Nine-thirty a.m.

While Nancy remained on the line, she pointed to Louise. "Call Harry Doyle. An ambulance and the sheriff are on their way. Harry needs to direct them to where we are."

Louise nodded and took out her cell phone.

Within a few moments, Harry had joined Nancy and Louise, and they watched the paramedics and sheriff's deputies handle the crime scene. Harry was white-faced and muttering to himself, "Not again. Not again."

Nancy was feeling the same way. Once more, she had brought the sheriff's deputies out to a crime scene at Whisperwood, a quiet, nonviolent place that one thousand residents called home.

Who could have shot Alex Elmo? No one here knew him except his grandparents. Harry Doyle would have to tell them. They'd be devastated. Alex was their only grandchild. His Great-Aunt Glinda had not been a popular person at Whisperwood. She'd been murdered by criminals because she knew too much. Alex was searching for Glinda's steamer trunk. What could be so important about Glinda's old steamer trunk? An antique, but not worth murdering for was Nancy's view.

The sheriff took down their names and contact information, and then asked about the victim's next of kin. "I gotta go talk to them," the sheriff said. "Worst part of my job."

Harry gave him Barbara and Don's apartment number. Nancy and Harry walked back to the building and paused in the reception area.

"You should stop by Barbara and Don's after the sheriff leaves," Nancy told Harry. "See if they need anything and suggest counseling. The people here are elderly. When they die, their family is halfway expecting the news. This is different."

Harry moaned. "I guess you're right."

"Would you like me to go with you?" Nancy asked. "In case extra support is needed?"

Harry looked at her gratefully. "Would you? I'm not good at handling situations like this."

Nancy nodded as she realized Harry was afraid he'd again be found inadequate to the task of Whisperwood administrator. His position had proven much more challenging than any of them expected.

Violet, the new life enrichment director, poked her head out of the office suite door. "What's going on?" she asked.

Harry explained and she joined them in the lobby. "That's awful," she said. "Are you sure he was shot?"

Nancy shuddered. "We're sure."

"But why?" Violet asked, looking from Nancy to Harry. "He didn't even live here, did he?"

"His grandparents live here," Nancy said. "His Great Aunt Glinda also lived here, but she was killed a year ago."

"His Great Aunt Glinda?" Violet said, her eyes opened wide. "He was her nephew?"

"Did you know her before you came here?" asked Nancy.

"I've heard the name," Violet said.

"He came here to get her old brassbound trunk," Nancy said, "but nobody knows where it is."

The portico entrance door opened and Sterling Cooper stalked in. "What in blazes is going on out there? Police cars, ambulance. Somebody hurt?"

Harry explained the situation to him as Sterling's eyes roved from face to face and stopped at Violet's a few seconds before moving on. Nancy noticed but dismissed his interest as only natural. Violet was an attractive woman, after all.

"You're telling me Alex was killed? Shot?" Sterling exclaimed. They nodded. Sterling stared down at the floor for a moment, muttering, "The trunk. It's got to be about that trunk."

"Is he talking about the trunk everyone wants?" asked Violet, her eyes wide with interest. "The one no one can find?"

"Yes," Nancy said.

Sterling stared at Violet. "I know you from someplace," he said.

Violet shrugged. "I've been in show business. You probably saw me in the theater."

"Could be. I managed Glinda Spencer's career," Sterling said. "You may have heard of her?"

Violet waved a hand. "Vaguely," Violet said with distaste.

Whatever Sterling heard in Violet's tone, he ignored it. "That trunk is mine," he said. "Make no mistake about it." He turned on his heel and left.

Nancy mulled over Violet's comment about Glinda. She sensed bad feeling there. History. Violet had not liked Glinda." But then, thought Nancy, neither had I.

A half-hour later, Harry and Nancy knocked on the door of the Elmos' apartment. Barbara Elmo opened it and invited them in. The pine smell of a disinfectant cleaner permeated the apartment, and the white furnishings and walls made the place seem unpleasantly sterile.

Barbara's face was stained with tears, and she

clenched a tissue. Don sat on the couch, looking at his hands. "We don't have time for visitors," Barbara said, and then she noticed their sad faces. "You heard?"

"Yes," said Nancy. "We are so sorry for your loss."

Don looked up from the armchair. "We don't know anything about that old steamer trunk," he said.

"They're not here about that," Barbara told him. "They know about Alex." She sat down on the couch next to him.

Harry stepped forward. "Would you like to talk to our counseling team?" he asked.

Barbara shook her head. "He'll never have a second chance now," she sobbed, her head resting on Don's chest.

"All he needed was a little luck," mumbled Don, hugging Barbara, "but he didn't even get that." His face had turned red with anger and then became grim.

Nancy and Harry had no answers for Barbara and Don and very little information to impart, but it wouldn't have helped if they did. Nancy again tendered their condolences and assurances that the sheriff was on the case and left.

"I hope they don't sue Whisperwood," Harry muttered as they walked back to his office.

Nancy's thoughts were on Sterling Cooper, Glinda's ex-husband, who had arrived the day before and was also seeking the steamer trunk. Where had he been when Alex was killed?

***

That evening the 90s Club met as usual at their favorite table for dinner and quickly gave the server their choices. Nancy surveyed the dining room, but as she expected, Barbara and Don did not appear. Bella spotted her and waved while Vicki looked on with a frown. Nancy's new neighbor, Caroline Richards, stopped by their table, and Nancy introduced her to the 90s Club. She was heavily made up as usual, and she wore an elegant black dress.

"Do you like it?" she asked as she pirouetted. "It's from the thrift shop." She paused. "People here have been telling me a lot about you," she said. "It's good you were on the job. You saved Whisperwood. Is this your regular table?"

"Yes," said Nancy, hoping she wouldn't ask to join them. "How are you settling in?"

"Loving it," Caroline said. "Nice meeting all of you." She moved on to a table across the room.

George, resplendent in a green and blue striped jacket and yellow slacks, toyed with the fish he'd ordered. He seemed in a contemplative mood. "Whisperwood has got to be above the national average in murders committed per one thousand residents," he said.

"Seems so," Louise commented, "but it's better than it was under the last administration."

"I feel so sorry for Barbara and Don," Nancy commented, "losing their only grandson." She took a sip of wine. "I did find out something about him that changes the picture somewhat."

George looked up. "What could that be?"

Nancy took a piece of bread, buttered it, and popped it into her mouth. She looked up to see all of them looking at her.

"All right, Nancy," Louise said. "What about

Alex Elmo?"

"He was a convicted felon," said Nancy. "Armed robbery. He'd just gotten out of prison six months ago."

"A convicted felon?" Louise's voice rose. "Here?"

"We've had worse," Nancy said. "I looked him up online in one of the databases I subscribe to." What she had found explained the Elmos' cryptic comments when they'd heard the news.

"I'm surprised," said Fitz. "The Elmos seem like such a conventional couple, but as with most of the couples we meet here, we don't know anything about their families."

"Alex could have gotten into drugs," said Nancy.

"I'm sure his grandparents didn't kill him," said Fitz. "And none of us did."

"We can rule out Harry Doyle, too," added Louise. "I saw him this afternoon. The sheriff was talking to him, and Harry looked green in the gills. Anyway, he was very upset when he saw the body this morning."

"I'll tell you who my Number One suspect is," said Nancy.

"Who?' asked Louise as the others stared at her.

"Nancy is always ahead of the rest of us." Fitz lifted his wine glass in a salute to her.

"I've been in the right place at the right time," Nancy demurred. "Yesterday, I was coming in from outside when a stranger walked up and we started talking. Turns out he was Glinda's ex-husband —"

George snorted. "I can't believe anyone would marry that obnoxious, self-centered gasbag," he said .

"Somebody did," Louise said, "and she had two kids. You told us about him. He was searching for Glinda's trunk, too."

"That's right. His name is Sterling Cooper." Nancy looked at them over her wine glass. "He claimed he'd loaned it to Glinda, and it belonged to him."

"That's two people looking for Glinda's trunk," Fitz said. "One of them was killed. The obvious suspect is the other one."

"Do we know anything else about him?" asked George.

"He said he was her manager," Nancy added, "and he told me—you'll not believe this—she was called 'The Singing Canary.'" She laughed.

Louise choked. George shook his head.

"Have you told the sheriff about him?" asked Fitz, ever sensible.

Nancy nodded. "I called the sheriff's office to offer our help and mentioned that Sterling Cooper might have information of interest and that he was staying at the motel down the road."

Louise snorted. "And what did the sheriff say?"

Nancy waved a hand. "He brushed me off."

"Usual response." George lifted his glass. "Onward!"

"Onward!" The others said and drank to the toast.

Another mystery to solve, Nancy thought as she contemplated three questions. Who had killed Alex Elmo? Where was the steamer trunk? Why did Alex and Sterling want it?

Nancy and Fitz returned to her apartment after dinner, hand in hand. When they entered, Fitz looked around and then walked to the phone. He took it apart. "Nothing," he said.

"What are you doing?" asked Nancy.

"Searching for bugs," Fitz whispered in her ear as he examined a lamp. "Yesterday I felt something was wrong here. I think someone got in despite Malone, but why? I thought they may have planted a bug, but I haven't found one yet." He shrugged.

"Anyway, how would they get in past Malone?" asked Nancy. "He'd tear them apart."

Letter to the Administrator and All Residents from a Concerned Citizen
What is being done about increasing security at Whisperwood? Now I hear someone has been murdered on the grounds. Shameful. We deserve to live worry-free and safe in our retirement. I demand an answer.

Alma Mead, concerned citizen and
Whisperwood resident

Chapter 5

Fitz left early the next morning to play pickleball with a group rapidly becoming fanatics about the new game. One of Whisperwood's two tennis courts had been transformed into a pickleball court and a debate was ongoing about whether it should stay that way.

Nancy finished breakfast and was drinking her second cup of tea as she watched Malone pace back and forth like a caged lion, growling and occasionally stopping and sniffing at the crack under the front door. I'll have to line up a play date with Cleo soon, she thought.

Then she heard a loud rap. "Just a minute," she called out as she picked up a treat from the kitchen and lured Malone into the bedroom. She left him engrossed in the treat, closed the bedroom door, and answered the knock to face a middle-aged man in a neat gray suit and red tie holding a clipboard.

"I'm Lt. Harmason, sheriff's office, ma'am." He pulled out his wallet and showed Nancy a badge and I.D. card. "Are you Nancy Dickinson?"

"Yes, I am." Nancy invited him in.

"I need to confirm and elaborate on the statement you gave the sheriff."

"Of course. My friend Louise was with me then. Shall I call and have her join us?"

Harmason shook his head and referred to the clipboard. "That's Louise Owens? I'll talk to her separately later."

Nancy understood. He wanted their different viewpoints, not a collaborated account. "I'll be glad to help you however I can," Nancy said.

"Good. How did you happen to find the body?"

"Louise and I were walking on the grounds and saw Alex leaning against the shed. We went over to talk to him and discovered he'd been shot."

"Did you touch the body or in any way change the scene? Move anything?"

"We saw the bullet hole in his chest. He wasn't moving or bleeding. We knew we couldn't help, so we backed away and called 911. Then we notified Harry Doyle, who is Whisperwood administrator, and stayed on the scene until the sheriff came."

"Did you know anything about the victim?"

"We knew he was the grandson of residents here." Nancy paused. Should she mention Glinda? "He was looking for a steamer trunk that had belonged to his great aunt, a former resident here, now deceased."

Harmason wasn't taking many notes or he wrote in shorthand. Maybe he was dismissing her comments as irrelevant. "Would you like a cup of coffee?" she asked. "Or tea?"

He looked at her with a slight smile. "No, ma'am. What about that steamer trunk? Was it valuable?"

"Not very, I should think," said Nancy. "It could be an antique, but it wasn't in good condition. As I told the sheriff, someone else has shown up, too, to ask about it, the former owner's ex-husband."

"You're saying both the victim and the ex-husband wanted the old steamer trunk. Why?"

Nancy shrugged. "We don't know. You'll have to ask him."

"Does anyone have the trunk?"

Nancy shook her head. "No one knows where it is."

He pursed his lips as he stared at her without expression. He referred back to his notes. "Is there anything else you can tell me about the victim?" he asked.

"One more thing, which might be irrelevant."

"Nevertheless..."

"Alex's great aunt, the one who owned the steamer trunk, was murdered here a year ago, but the killers were caught."

"Yes, ma'am. I've read the case files. You and your 90s Club were on the scene and happened to find out what was going on here." He stood somewhat defensively. "However, Ms. Dickinson, catching killers is not your job or that of any of your friends. Stay out of this investigation. It is dangerous work and not for you, uh, senior citizens, ma'am."

Honeyed words were not Nancy's style. Her eyes narrowed at his presumption. As she walked him to the door, she coldly replied, "We step in to help when we're needed, officer."

Would the man see the words as the slap in the face they were intended to be? Probably not.

He turned a stern face to her. "Your services are not required, ma'am."

She closed the door behind him, then let Malone out of the bedroom before calling Louise to alert her to Harmason's visit. She didn't relay Harmason's parting words because Louise would turn hostile against the man, and they needed to appear friendly and helpful.

A few minutes later, the phone rang. Nancy answered it with a brisk "Hello?"

"Good morning, Ms. Dickenson," Ashley said in formal tones. Harry had been training her in good front desk manners. "Mr. Cooper is here to see you. Shall I give him your apartment number?"

A vision of the scrawny Alaskan surfaced. Sterling Cooper. Glinda's ex-husband. She'd rather keep him at arm's length.

"I'll be right down," she said. "Tell him to wait there."

Again she found a piece of fish in the refrigerator to entice Malone away from the door, then scooted out to the hall, closing the door securely behind her. She heard Malone scratching at the door and snarling.

Sterling Cooper sat in one of the comfortable armchairs with a cup of coffee from the lobby's coffee bar. He stood and waved the cup at her as she approached. "Thanks for coming down to talk with me," he said.

"Glad to," said Nancy. "Were you able to help the sheriff?"

He shrugged. "He considers me a suspect, but I haven't seen any of these people for twenty years, at least. I didn't even know Glinda was dead until a few weeks ago when I read it in the Anchorage newspaper.

Why would I want to kill Alex Elmo?"

"Why all the interest in her steamer trunk?" Nancy countered. "That seems to be what you and Alex were after."

"Oh that," Sterling said. He waved his hand as if the trunk were of no consequence. Nancy waited.

"A keepsake. A memory." He sighed. "That's why I wanted to talk to you. I gave it to Glinda when I was madly in love with her. That was years ago. I was much younger then and didn't care much about my family heritage. Since she moved away with a lot of my family things, I've realized that I want them back, that's all. They belong to my family. You can see how much her sister and sons care about that old trunk. They don't even know where it is."

"I see," said Nancy. "How did you find out Glinda had died?"

"She was well-known in Alaska. 'The Singing Canary,' you know. Local newspapers picked up the story about her recently and how she was murdered. I just happened to come across it. Stirred up a lot of memories. Of course, I was interested."

"So why did Alex Elmo want the trunk, too?" Nancy asked.

"Have no idea. It was brassbound and looked fancy. Probably thought he could get some money for it." He stopped to sip his coffee. "Out for every dime he could get. That was Alex. Can't figure out why else he'd want such a thing. He was a low-life." He took a sip. "But, hey, I hadn't seen him since he was a kid. Maybe he turned out okay."

"The question is moot, anyway," Nancy said,

"since no one knows where it is."

"I'm going to be hanging around a few weeks," said Sterling. "I'll probably run into you again. If you find it, I hope you'll let me know. I'm the rightful owner of that trunk and I want it back. Now I've got to go visit Barbara and Don and give them my condolences for that worthless grandson of theirs." Nancy rose as he did.

"Good luck in your search," she said as she shook his hand.

***

She met Louise later in the Pub for lunch. In a far corner, she saw Sterling hunched over a book, eating by himself. "I talked to Sterling this morning," she told Louise, nodding toward him. "Glinda's ex."

Louise turned around and spotted him. "What did you find out?" she asked.

"He said the trunk was an heirloom from his family that he gave to Glinda."

"Trying to establish his claim." Louise flicked her long braid behind her back. The button she wore said, "Do Your Part."

"I suppose so," agreed Nancy. "What do you think happened to that trunk?"

"Probably in a dump somewhere," Louise said and hailed a server.

"BLT and iced tea for me," Nancy said as the server stood by their table, pen in hand.

"Ditto," said Louise.

She watched the server flounce back to the bar. "I usually order at the bar," she said to Nancy, "but you had already taken a table, and I'm in no hurry. Thanks for alerting me to the visit from Deective Harmason."

"How did it go?" Nancy asked.

"Swimmingly until he warned me about us doing any investigating. They would be wiser to use our inside information. Make us part of the team."

"He's a new investigator. Haven't met him before," Nancy said. "He warned me, too."

"Now what?"

Nancy leaned toward Louise to keep her voice down. "Remember in our first case here at Whisperwood, we ran into residents wondering where they misplaced their jewelry, watches, and other things? They thought they were losing their minds, but actually, a thief was at work here."

Simon Smythe, a long-time resident, happened to pass by at that moment. "Thieves?" he said, stopping at their table. "Nonsense. Nobody's stealing anything here. This place is full of half-addled geezers who forget where they put their heads. Don't waste your time. That trunk of Glinda's is rotting away in some trash pile, mark my words." He rapped his knuckles on the table and walked on.

"I don't think so," said Nancy as he retreated. "Louise, you and now Simon say the trunk was dumped. "I'm betting it's hidden somewhere in this building."

Security Team Expands Patrols

In light of the recent tragedy at Whisperwood, Security Chief Charles W. Beale is adding new staff and additional patrols to its security efforts at Whisperwood. He

will be discussing the new safety measures and ways you can protect yourself
in his talk on Wednesday, 10 a.m., in the
Dining Room. Please plan to attend and
bring your questions.

The Whisperwood Breeze,
Newsletter of the Whisperwood
Retirement Village

Chapter 6

Nancy left Louise after lunch to visit Barbara and Don Elmo. A black wreath hung on their door. Barbara didn't look pleased to see Nancy but invited her in.

"Shh," she said. "Don's taking a nap. I can't sleep thinking of my poor boy."

Barbara gestured to the sofa and took the armchair. "What do you want?" she asked.

Nancy got to the point, recognizing the lack of friendliness from Barbara and the need to keep her voice down for Don. "I'm very sorry about your grandson," she said.

Barbara stared at her hands. "Thank you."

"I met him. He seemed like a nice young man. He asked me about Glinda's steamer trunk, the brass-bound one. No one seems to know where it is," Nancy said. "Glinda also had a Tiffany lamp and a Russian boundary plaque from Alaska. Nobody has seen the plaque, but Cary took the lamp to the thrift shop downstairs. He thought it was fake. I talked to Paige Lincoln who runs the shop, and she did, too."

Barbara snorted. "Sure it was fake. Like everything else about Glinda."

Nancy disagreed, but the lamp had been sold as part of a boxed lot and that was that. "What about the boundary plaque? Do you have it?"

Barbara shook her head. "That plaque belonged in a museum, not in her boudoir."

Nancy agreed. "What happened to it?"

"How should I know? Ask Cary."

A groan issued from the bedroom. Barbara stood. "I can't help you," she said and led Nancy out the door and into the hall. Barbara closed the door behind her.

"Wait a minute," she said. "I need to talk to you, somewhere privately."

"Now?" Nancy asked.

"Yes, now. Where can we go?"

Fitz was busy with a birdhouse project in their apartment. "What about the library on the fifth floor?" she said. "It's usually free this time of day."

"All right, let's go."

They arrived at the library as the lone browser was leaving. They took the table next to the window behind the bookstacks.

"What's up?" asked Nancy.

"We all know about the crimes you've solved since you moved here," said Barbara belligerently. One hand gripped the other in her lap. Tears hovered in her eyes, but she held her head up and frowned at Nancy.

She's going to ask for help and hates the idea, thought Nancy.

"You used to be a private detective," Barbara added and swallowed. "I...we need your help. Don didn't want me to ask you, but our boy was...murdered."

Nancy saw Barbara's jaw tighten and her hands shake. How hard it was for her to say that. "The 90s Club is already looking into this...crime."

"Thank you," Barbara whispered. "The sheriff and his deputies are on the job, but none of them know what goes on here. They weren't the ones who solved Glinda's murder. The 90s Club did that."

"And don't forget Malone," added Nancy. She owed her life to her cantankerous cat. Twice.

"Of course."

"Why do you think Alex was looking for Glinda's brassbound trunk?" asked Nancy. "What happened to it?"

"Have no idea. You should take a close look at her ex, Sterling Cooper. He is after the trunk, too. Why after all this time?"

"Did you move here from Alaska?" asked Nancy.

"That's where Glinda and I grew up. I married Don and Glinda and I went our separate ways." Barbara's eyes narrowed in disgust. "She became 'The Singing Canary,' I guess you've heard. I lived in Anchorage and raised my son there. He did all right, but his son, our grandson, Alex, was always a handful. He went to the university in Fairbanks, but he got in with a bad crowd and didn't graduate. He's been drifting since. I was glad to see him here. We were talking about him going to the university in Morgantown where he could be close to his cousins."

Barbara choked back a sob. "That won't happen now." She covered her eyes for a moment.

Nancy waited until Barbara brought her hands

down to the table. "The steamer trunk was from Alaska. What could have happened to bring both Alex and Sterling Cooper down here to search for it? It couldn't have been worth much."

"You'll have to ask Sterling," Barbara said bitterly. "He's the one who should have been killed, not Alex. Sterling is a conniving..." She paused to collect herself. "We want to know who murdered our grandson in cold blood and why. We want the killer punished. Alex was beginning to find himself. No one had the right to kill him."

"We are all concerned and want to see justice done. The 90s Club is working on the case."

Barbara wiped her eyes. "Thank you," she said. "Please don't let anyone know I asked you to do this. Don will be angry if he finds out."

"No need for him to learn anything about it," Nancy assured her.

***

At dinner that evening, Nancy shared Barbara's request with the other 90s Club members, Fitz, Louise, and George. The chardonnay had been poured and their meals ordered.

Nancy wore blue slacks with a cream-colored, long-sleeved shirt. Fitz was in jeans and a blue short-sleeved shirt. George's outfit tonight was a lime green suit with a pink tie. He usually garnered second and third looks as he passed through the dining room on the way to their table, but this time, people covered their eyes from the glare.

"We know you love color," commented Louise, "and that outfit is true to form."

Nancy glanced at her in surprise, Louise's voice was softer and the comment kinder than her usual sarcasm. Perhaps she was worried about the competition from Bella Shore. Then Nancy stole a look at George who appeared oblivious.

Louise flicked her long, gray braid. The button on her white polo shirt said, "Plant for Butterflies and Bees." She sat back and surveyed the table with a smile. "All present and accounted for, I see."

The server took their orders and left. Looking across the dining room, Nancy spotted Caroline sitting with Barbara and Don Elmo. Caroline seemed to be listening intently to every word Barbara spoke.

"Here's something we need to consider," began Fitz. "Both Alex and Sterling Cooper were interested in finding Glinda's trunk. Was Axel murdered because of the trunk? Maybe he found out where it is, but if that was the reason for killing him, then Sterling Cooper might be the next victim unless he is the murderer himself."

"We should point this out to Cooper," said Louise. "I don't think he's realized that yet."

"If he's not being careful," added George, "then maybe he is the murderer." He picked up his napkin and shook out the silverware as their food arrived.

Nancy reached for the salt. "We've got to find the brassbound trunk," she said. "That's the key to what's been happening here."

"Why Does Sterling Cooper want it?" added Fitz. "Who is he, other than Glinda's ex-husband?"

"Now that we're unofficially on the case," said Louise, "so to speak, Nancy needs to check her databases and find out more about Sterling Cooper and Alex. They could both be wanted criminals, for all we know."

"I found out Alex was a convicted felon," said Nancy. "I should have done the same check on Sterling when we first met, especially with his ties to Glinda, who was not our most savory resident."

"That's the truth," muttered George under his breath.

Nancy dug into her mashed potatoes. "I'll do that when I get back to the room."

"After dinner," said Fitz, "I'll call Sterling at his motel and arrange to meet him for breakfast tomorrow." He glanced at George. "You want to join us?"

"Be glad to. What are we gonna ask him?" George set down his wine glass and reached for a roll.

"What he's doing here and why he wants the trunk," said Nancy. "He told me the trunk belongs to him. It's a family heirloom and he wants it back. See what kind of answers you get."

"What if he stonewalls us?" asked George as he took a pat of butter.

"Start by asking him about himself," suggested Louise. "Prime the pump. Men go for talking about themselves. How does he like our fair city? What's he doing in West Virginia? What did he do in Alaska? How long will he be staying? I got a million questions I could ask." She sat back and sipped her wine.

Nancy smiled at the self-satisfied look on Louise's face. "Anything you find out will be more than we know now," Nancy said, "But I'll do an Internet search while Fitz is calling. After Fitz and Sterling leave for breakfast, I'll ask Harry to let me look in the storage bays in the basement. He has the keys to those rooms."

"I'll go with you. The room for the residents' storage bays isn't locked," Louise said.

Nancy nodded. "That's right, but Whisperwood also has storage rooms for supplies, linens, and other necessary items, and they are kept locked. We need to look through those, too."

"I'll bet there's still stuff left over from the old administration," George added, referring to the crooks who had built Whisperwood.

They finished their dinners and waited for dessert. Louise glanced from Nancy to Fitz, then she brought them all to attention by tapping her fork on her glass. "Now for something really important," she said.

"What?" asked Nancy.

"I'm getting tired of waiting." Louise set down her fork and frowned at Nancy. "It's more than time enough. When are you two going to get married?" She drew herself up and stabbed a finger at Nancy. "And don't think you're going to elope."

Nancy glanced at Fitz. "We just want a quiet ceremony," she said. "Just the four of us. We're not in a rush."

Louise stared at her in disbelief. "Why not? We're all over ninety, for Pete's sake. Time's a'wastin'."

"I've been wondering that myself, Luv," put in Fitz. "Been waiting for you to come up with a date."

"You've got to go on a honeymoon, too," said Louise, "to make it official."

Nancy laughed and laid her hand on Fitz's as she

smiled at him. "What do you think?"

Fitz returned the smile. "We've taken on a new case. I say we get married as soon as we've solved it."

"That's settled then." Louise raised her glass. "Salud!"

After the toast, Louise grinned and sat back. "The only decision left is where we're all going for the honeymoon."

An Invitation

Whisperwood's beautiful nondenominational chapel can be booked for any private religious event from baby christenings to bar mitzvahs. If romance is in the air, the chapel staff will assist you in preparing the wedding of your dreams with an officiant of your choice. After the ceremony, celebrate with your friends with a catered dinner in the private dining room. To make arrangements, contact Violet Velois, 304-555-6780.

The Whisperwood Breeze,
Newsletter of Whisperwood
Retirement Village

Chapter 7

After dinner, Fitz called Sterling and arranged to meet for breakfast in town. Nancy spent an hour searching the names of Sterling Cooper and Alex Elmo through Google and her crime databases. The search turned out to be an eye-opener. She knew that Alex was a convicted felon, but both men had served prison time for shoplifting, smuggling, and burglary, although there were no outstanding warrants.

Sterling Cooper had held various backstage jobs in theaters. That's probably how he met Glinda, thought Nancy. Another search showed that Alex had worked on fishing boats when he wasn't at the university—or in jail.

Both men had criminal backgrounds, both were connected with Glinda, and both coveted Glinda's brassbound trunk. Why? Nancy had seen the trunk. It looked like junk to her. The value must be in something it contained. The Russian boundary plaque? But that was long gone. When Glinda had shown Nancy the trunk, she had taken out the plaque, leaving the trunk empty. Could it have a secret bottom or other hidden compartment? If so, what did it hide?

Glinda had lived and worked in Alaska. People in Alaska joked about being able to see Russia across the Bering Sea. Alex had worked on a fishing boat. Fishing boats in the Bering Sea could venture close to Russia and connect with ships from all over the Pacific. Her imagination brought up visions of smugglers hiding drugs, ivory, gemstones, rhino horns, and other illegal items in a trunk aboard a fishing boat or, in fact, any boat. Passengers had used steamer trunks for long sea voyages in the past. Would those trunks have hidden compartments for contraband? Wouldn't customs agents look for those?

Was any kind of smuggling trade going on between Alaska and Russia? She Googled the question and found an item about two Americans indicted for trying to smuggle snowmobiles into Russia. Nancy supposed that smuggling other luxury items both ways might be possible. Caviar from Russia to America, for instance. It still seemed unlikely to Nancy, but the question remained. Why did Alex and Sterling want Glinda's brassbound trunk? She smiled as she thought of Glinda trying to stuff a snowmobile into the trunk.

Nancy checked her watch. Only eight-thirty. She called Glinda's son Cary. He answered.

"Sorry to bother you again, but I have one question. Did your mother ever travel out of the country?"

Cary chuckled. "What an odd question. Maybe you're thinking that old trunk was full of hidden drugs."

"No, no," Nancy laughed. "Nothing like that. She had a steamer trunk. Did she like to travel?"

"She had costumes, you know," Cary said. "But she was xenophobic and had no interest in foreign anything. She limited her traveling to 'good ol' USA'."

"I see. Thank you." After a few more pleasantries, Nancy signed off.

Glinda was a mediocre entertainer. How did she earn enough to afford an apartment in this expensive retirement village? Alex and Sterling were both crooks. Could the three of them have worked together in a smuggling racket? The trunk could be unfinished business, perhaps still hiding smuggled items worth big money. That would explain Alex and Sterling's interest in finding the trunk.

Then, on a whim, she searched the Internet for what she could find on Whisperwood's new employee, Violet Velois. Violet was listed on LinkedIn, promoting herself as an event manager and talent agent with a brief reference to her past career as a blues singer in Chicago. Her website featured a short bio and rave reviews on her clients. Her photo on both sites depicted the businesswoman they had met at Whisperwood. Nancy wondered what she'd look like made up as a glamorous and sultry blues singer.

The new finance director, Gene Reynolds with his wife and kids, seemed like an open book and didn't interest Nancy.

She relayed Violet's background to Fitz. He whistled. "I can see that," he said. "I'll bet she's a beauty when she lets her hair down. She's playing a role, isn't she?"

"Quite," said Nancy. "Being an entertainer in Chicago would be a sophisticated and exciting whirlwind.

Why would she want to move to our backwater town and work at Whisperwood?"

Fitz nodded. "Sounds strange to me, Luv." Fitz sat in his favorite easy chair with Malone in his lap. "Maybe she needed to hide out. She bears watching."

Nancy marveled at the way Malone lapped up the attention from Fitz and kept his claws withdrawn. For now, Malone had stopped pacing and growling at the door.

Fitz lazily stroked the cat and smiled at Nancy. "What do you think?" he asked.

"About what?" Nancy had turned back to her computer.

"Do you want a church wedding or a justice of the peace?"

Nancy closed the laptop. "I've had two church weddings," she said. "I'm done. George loves ceremony. He can easily get a divinity license online to marry us. I want a small affair that is fun."

"That sounds good to me," said Fitz. "We can ask George tomorrow and start taking care of whatever we need to do to get married the day after we solve the case." He looked at Nancy for confirmation.

"All right," she said and high-fived him. "Where shall we go for a honeymoon?"

Fitz laughed. "George and Louise expect to come, too."

"I wouldn't mind. Would you?" Nancy walked over to the armchair, sat on the wide, upholstered arm, and kissed Fitz on the forehead.

Malone hissed, jumped down with a put-upon look, and stalked out of the room.

"No, but our choice gets priority." Fitz reached up and pulled her into his arms.

***

The next morning, Nancy saw Fitz and George off to join Sterling for breakfast. She was meeting Louise at nine in the lobby and arrived early to pick up a cup of coffee and read her book. She was sipping coffee comfortably in a lobby armchair when she saw Louise tramp through the front door in her white beekeeping suit and boots. Louise held the netted hat and heavy yellow gloves in one hand.

"Nancy, I got to talk to you." Louise looked harried. "You won't believe what I got to tell you." She glanced at Ashley, all ears at the reception desk. "Let's go outside."

"What's up?" asked Nancy as they walked out the door.

"Geesh," Louise shook her head. "You know I like George."

"Of course. We all do," said Nancy. *What had George done now?*

"Yeah, but not enough to marry him. I like my life the way it is. I don't have to answer to anybody."

"What?" Nancy stopped to process. "George has asked you to marry him?"

"Sure has. Last night. After dinner. We were walking back to our apartments, and it just popped out. What am I gonna do, Nancy?"

"I thought you and George were friends. What happened?"

"You and Fitz getting married." Louise picked up a branch and swung it in a joking gesture. "I'll tell you, Nancy, you might ruin us all."

Nancy turned a mischievous smile on Louise. "I gather you don't want to marry George."

"Absolutely not."

"We all like George. I hope your refusal won't affect our relationship," said Nancy. George was quirky and he grumbled a lot, but he was lovable in his way, and the 90s Club needed his computer skills. "I guess we'll see how he's taking this at dinner tonight," she finally said. *Poor George.*

Nancy glanced at the front door and saw Harry wave at them as he bounced into the building, whistling.

"Harry's here," she said. "We can get the keys to Whisperwood's supply rooms now." They walked back into the building to see Harry unlock the door to the executive suite and disappear into his office.

"Wait a minute." Louise sat in one of the lobby couches and held up her cup. "Let me finish my coffee and change my clothes."

Nancy filled a cup for herself from the coffee bar and waited for Louise.

A short while later, Vicki and Bella, the two sisters who had recently moved into Whisperwood, stopped on their way through the lobby toward the portico door.

"Hello," gushed Bella. "We've been hoping to bump into you." She flounced into the chair across from Nancy and smoothed the ruffled hem of her dress.

'We'd like to get to know you better," said Vicki, pulling up another chair. She wore jeans and a long-sleeved blouse. "We'd love to hear about your detecting adventures."

Nancy glanced at Louise who had joined them and was intent on ignoring the sisters, but Nancy felt the need to be polite. "We aren't really detectives..." she began.

"People have been telling us about the crimes you've solved here," said Bella. "We want to meet your sweet little kitty cat, too. People here rave about him."

Nancy choked and heard Louise chuckle.

"Yeah, Nancy," said Louise, grinning at Nancy. "You ought to let them meet Malone."

The sisters looked at Nancy expectantly, but Nancy knew that Malone drew blood and would likely rip Bella's stockings to shreds, leaving her legs bloody stumps. "He doesn't take to visitors," she said.

"All right, but we do want to become friends, so Bella talked to the dining room manager," said Vicki. "She asked him to set us up with the four of you at dinner."

"He said he'd put us all at a table for six," added Bella. "Only you need to tell him you agree. We didn't think there would be any problem with that."

Nancy stared at her while a dozen thoughts raced through her mind. *They mean well,* she thought, *trying to be kind, but I like meeting with the four of us, and we have important business to discuss. I don't think these two women will be helpful.* She glanced at Bella's baby doll face, which had taken on a greedy look. She had seen that look before when Bella had met George.

She glanced at Louise who frowned back at her.

Nancy understood. They shared the same thought. The two sisters had an ulterior motive. Could Bella be serious about George? Or were they also interested in Glinda's trunk? She cast about for a way to refuse without hurting their feelings.

Louise had no such scruples. "Sorry," she said. "No can do. The four of us have important business to conduct and we do that at dinner. Right now we are addressing a multitude of concerns, including murder and theft."

Vicki's face showed no expression except a slight smile at the opposition to the plan. Bella's face turned red with suppressed anger.

"We are offering to help," spit out Bella. "We have experience you could use."

"What kind of experience do you mean?" asked Nancy.

"I'm a people person," said Bella. "I can talk to the suspects, dig out the dirt about them."

"I've some experience in the field," said Vicki.

"I see..." ventured Nancy.

"Good. We'll keep you in mind when we need your...skills," added Louise with finality. "Right now, we don't."

"If that's the way you feel..." Bella sniffed. She rose, pulling Vicki along with her, but Nancy saw Vicki hide a smile as if the refusal was a relief. Maybe it was.

Bella walked in a huff with her sister out the front door into the sunlight.

"The nerve," said Louise. "Good riddance."

Nancy said nothing, still conflicted, but Louise

jumped up. "Time to get the supply room keys."

Harry was the only executive office staff member in this early, so they walked directly into his office. Nancy explained their mission.

"Okay," he said. "I don't think you'll find anything, but I wish you good luck."

He gave them the keys and returned to his desk and the stack of bills confronting him. He didn't look up when he waved goodbye.

Nancy and Louise took the elevator to the basement. They walked down the hall past the classrooms, the art studio with its display windows, and the woodworking shop. They came to a double-wide door, which was unlocked. It opened into a large space of four-foot-square wire cages stacked two deep for residents' storage. Each cubicle had a lock on its door.

They examined these storage cubicles first, going down the aisles and marveling at the accumulated junk revealed through the wire fencing. They found no brassbound trunk, which would have been hard to hide, but the Russian plaque could have been buried inside any of the boxes filling up the units.

They left the residents' storage area and unlocked Whisperwood's supply room. It yielded only common hotel necessities, nothing suspicious, and no trunk. Boxes were labeled and when Nancy opened up one or two, the contents were as labeled.

"Nothing here," she said, turning to Louise.

They walked out, and Nancy locked the door behind them. Louise headed for the elevator.

"Wait," said Nancy, striding to the end of the hall.

Louise followed. "There's nothing down there

now," she said. "You don't think..."

Nancy stood, hands on hips, examining the dead end in front of her. "This wall hasn't been touched," she said. "It's still plywood painted to look like the other walls, and it still has a concealed door in it."

"It can't be. They closed everything up," said Louise, subconsciously rubbing her wrist.

Memories rushed through Nancy's mind. They had found that hidden door a year ago and used it to gain access to the tunnels below the building. They had almost lost their lives in the tunnels, remnants of a mining operation never cleaned up or rehabilitated.

Louise looked closer at the wall and whistled. "You're right. They brought the renovation crew in through the truck entrance on the other side of the building. Did they not know about this entrance? I find that hard to believe since they would have seen the stairs inside the tunnel that lead up to it."

Nancy looked at Louise. "Do you think everything has been cleaned up and the toxic materials removed? The construction crew was supposed to block off all the tunnels, too."

"I hate to say this," said Louise, "but we need to bring George and Fitz with his tools down here to look at this."

Nancy saw the fear flash across Louise's face. A year ago, when they encountered the killers at Whisperwood, they were left tied and in fear for their lives. Louise broke her wrist and endured hours of pain until they could escape. Her wrist still ached at times, but Louise was resilient and tough.

She examined the barely visible seams in the wall

in front of her. "I'll bet we can still open this hidden door," she said. "They've taken down the warning sign so we'll all think it's the end wall."

"We found a bin down in those tunnels a year ago," said Nancy, "where crooks had stashed items they'd stolen from the residents. The construction crews should have blocked off all access to those tunnels."

"This one got away," said Louise.

They looked at each other.

"The trunk?" said Nancy.

"The boundary plaque?" added Louise.

***

Nancy returned the keys to Harry and the two women took seats in the lobby armchairs to wait for Fitz and George.

"Harry doesn't have any idea what's going on in the tunnels," said Nancy. "He thinks they've all been filled in and are no longer a problem."

"He never did think there was a problem," said Louise. "He's good at day-to-day administering to the needs of Whisperwood and its residents, but he's still young and naive about us conniving senior citizens." She grinned and winked at Nancy.

"Here they come," said Nancy, watching as Fitz and George walked through the front door.

"Let's get coffee at the Pub," said Fitz, taking Nancy's arm as she stood.

"How did it go?" asked Louise.

"We got stuff to tell you," said George grimly. "Hold onto your hat."

"You'd better hold onto yours," Louise shot back.

**Special Notice to the Residents
Spring Clean Those Storage Bins!**
Whisperwood conducts annual inspections of the storage bin areas to look for hazardous situations and conditions that may attract rodents and insects. This inspection will be conducted next Monday between eight a.m. and noon. Please check your storage bin and discard any materials that will cause our monitors to give you a citation. Remember, if you haven't used it in a year, throw it out. Help keep our storage bins clean and safe.

Harry Doyle, Administrator

Chapter 8

They walked to the Pub and ordered coffee for three and one hot tea for Nancy. Fitz glanced at his watch. "We just finished breakfast and it's a bit early for lunch."

"Not for me," said Louise, as they selected a table in the far corner. She picked up a menu.

Despite his cheery greeting, George seemed more subdued than usual and avoided looking at Louise as he scanned the Pub for any listeners, saw none, and slapped the table. "The first thing Sterling said when we sat down in the cafe was, 'I didn't have nothing to do with that young man's death.'"

Fitz grinned. "He was nervous, and his hands were shaking."

"He was afraid of us," said George.

"Or somebody," added Fitz. "He was scared."

"We don't know why Alex was killed," said Nancy slowly, "but Sterling could have done it; if not, he may be the next victim."

Fitz nodded. "He has figured that out. He kept looking around the restaurant and wanted to sit away from a window with his back against a wall.."

"We told him we were trying to find out what this was all about," said George. "Why were both of them so interested in Glinda's brassbound trunk?"

"He tried to be cagey," George said, "but the man ain't that bright."

"He said he didn't know why Alex wanted the trunk except that he might think it was a valuable antique." Fitz stopped as their drinks were delivered. He drank his coffee black, so after taking a sip, he said, "Maybe so, and Alex probably could have used the money."

George broke in. "Then he said that Alex must have been looking for the Russian boundary plaque. That probably would have been worth something to somebody, maybe a museum. Alex could have thought the plaque was in the trunk."

"It seems to have disappeared," said Nancy, "along with the trunk."

"So why did Sterling want the trunk?" asked Louise.

George snorted. "Sentimental reasons he said. Reminded him of Glinda, his one true love." He sat back, his disbelief radiating. "Love for that obnoxious..."

"Simmer down," said Nancy. "We all know love is blind."

"I guess so," said George, looking at Louise.

Fitz chuckled. "They'd been divorced a long time, though. Hard to believe he'd keep a flame alive that long. There must be something else."

"But what?" asked Louise.

They pondered the question a moment. Then Nancy said, "We won't learn that until we find the trunk."

"But we've asked everyone who might have found it," said George.

"While we were sitting in the cafe," said Fitz, "our new neighbor, Caroline something, came in. She saw us and stopped by our table,"

"She wanted to join us," added George with a wink. "I wouldn't have minded that. She's cute."

Nancy glanced at Louise, but except for a grim cast to her mouth, Louise ignored the remark.

Fitz shook his head. "Not going to happen. She went on to her table."

"While you were out," Nancy said. "Louise and I searched the storage bins in the basement. Nothing stood out as relevant."

"But are you ready for this?" asked Louise. "We've got an idea."

"Uh, oh," said George.

Nancy grinned and, noticing the server watching them, leaned forward to whisper, "Remember the fake door in the end wall of the basement?"

"I still have nightmares," George said with a shudder.

"So do I," said Louise, rubbing her wrist as she blurted. "They never took that door out."

Fitz drew back in horror. "It's still there?"

"Yes," whispered Nancy. "That means we can get into the tunnels under this building. They've probably blocked up most of them, but not the one directly under that door. It would be a great place to hide contraband or anything else."

"Like something secret," added Louise.

"Uh oh, I know where this is going," groaned

George, shaking his head.

Nancy nodded. "We need to explore what's down there."

George shook his head. "I knew it."

"We'll have to go late at night when no one's around," Fitz said. "What about the security guards?"

"One stays at the lobby reception desk and one makes the rounds in the building," said Nancy. "There's also one at the entrance gate and one who tours the grounds in a golf cart."

"Did you notice any cameras or guards in the basement?" asked Fitz.

"After being tied up and left for slaughter in one of those basement classrooms, I get the chills whenever I go near that end wall. I stay away." George shivered.

"Don't blame you," said Nancy. "I still take classes in the basement, but I never looked for cameras and never saw guards down there."

Louise took out a small notepad and wrote, "Item 1, find out how the basement is guarded. Cameras? Guard patrols?" She looked up expectantly, "So this afternoon, we can walk through the basement and look for cameras."

"All right," said Nancy. "I'll think of some excuse to ask the chief of security about how the guards work at night."

Fitz looked at her. "You'll have to be super careful, Luv. You don't want him thinking that maybe he should add guard rounds in the basement if residents are worried."

"You're right, but they expect such questions

from me." Nancy thoughtfully took another sip of tea.

Louise checked her watch. "Let's go down to the basement now and look for cameras." She saw George's expression and added, "You're excused, George."

"Good." He pushed back his chair. "I'm meeting some people for lunch."

"There is one thing you can do," Nancy said. "It's easy and won't take up much time."

"What's that?" George peered over his glasses.

"Go to the security guard offices and look at their monitors. You can find out where the cameras are located and what they're trained at."

"That's a good idea," said Fitz.

George nodded. "I'm a resident. I have a right to know."

Louise held up her hand. "Let's meet at three this afternoon in my apartment to plan exactly what we're going to do tonight. Nancy, you should have checked with the security chief by then, and..." She nodded at George. "George should know about the cameras."

Nancy nodded. "I'll tell the chief I'm writing an article for the newsletter. Then I'll take his picture."

"He's wise to us." Louise frowned. "He'll be suspicious. Better to tackle him after George has found out about the monitors and we've scouted out the tunnels."

"Why?" asked Nancy. "We need to know how they plan their patrols."

"Louise is right," put in Fitz. "If we try to find out what they're doing before we explore the tunnels, and they catch us, we'll be seen as sneaky and trying to one-up them. They'll give us the usual warnings and prohibitions. If we go afterward with findings they need and tell them we stumbled upon the findings accidentally, we can present ourselves as supporters of the security team and trying to help."

"I see." Nancy nodded. "Better we seem to be innocent residents who stumble upon activities and information they need..."

"But they know us as amateur detectives," objected Louise. "They know we're investigating."

George rapped on the table. "And they don't like it one bit."

"You're right." Nancy mulled over the possibilities. "But much better to be considered allies than enemies, right?"

"Right," agreed the other three.

What You Need to Know About Warning Signs and Signals

Please stay alert and pay attention to warning signs and signals, says Byron Farnsworth, Whisperwood's Chief of Security. "I am concerned that some of our more agile and curious residents may ignore warning signs and safety fences that limit access to hazardous places on the grounds. Ignoring these clear signals may result in injury or death, so please be heed the signs and be careful.

Chief Farnsworth notes that in the recent fire drill, announced in advance, many residents did not follow the correct procedure. These fire drills are for your safety during an emergency. Please pay attention and do as instructed.

The Whisperwood Breeze,
Newsletter of Whisperwood
Retirement Village

Chapter 9

Nancy, Louise, and Fitz finished lunch and left the Pub to take the elevator to the basement. They passed a classroom with students learning Arabic and the crafts room where watercolor artists daubed brushes of color onto large sheets of paper. Several people lifted their heads from painting pottery to smile at the threesome passing by. No one was in the woodworking room.

At the end of the hall, the three detectives studied the wall with hands on hips. Fitz took a closer look at both edges of the wall. "They laid a thick coating of plaster on top to cover the grain of the plywood," He whispered. "And painted it, of course."

Nancy could barely see the outlines of the door that had been there the year before with a false sign warning of high-voltage electrical equipment.

"I say..." Fitz tapped along the outline. "Someone has been tinkering..." He turned to Nancy and Louise. "You're right, and I think this door still opens."

"You mean someone's using it?" Louise pushed on the wall inside the outline. "It moves."

"Keep your voice down," cautioned Fitz.

"Who would want access to the tunnel under the building?" Nancy's first thought was of Harry Doyle, but it didn't seem to be his style, and he appeared to be shocked that someone might still be using the Whisperwood underground. She dismissed Harry. Who else? Why?

"I wish I'd brought my tool belt," Fitz said.

Nancy took his hand. "Now wouldn't be the right time to pursue this."

"Not with those classrooms full of people," added Louise. "Let's go back to my apartment and discuss this." She glanced at her watch. "George should show up in a few minutes."

They left the basement and went up the elevator to Louise's fourth-floor apartment with its delicate antique furniture and dainty teacups, all inherited and of little interest to Louise. "Gotta do something with all these antiques," she had grumbled, "since my daughter doesn't want them, I use them. If they break, too bad." She wore a "Recycle" button on her blue tee shirt.

George with all his allergies preferred Louise's apartment to Nancy's with its dust and cat dander. "What did you find out?" he asked as they seated themselves on the rickety antique living room furniture.

"The door in the basement that leads to the tunnel is still in use," blurted out Louise. She wasn't much for suspense.

"What? How can that be?" George asked. "Those tunnels were blocked."

"We don't know," said Fitz. "George, what did

you find out about the closed-circuit television monitors in the guard room?"

"I don't think those people get to talk about their work to many people," George said. "The guy watching the monitors sure opened up to me. I was there over an hour."

Louise twirled her hand. "So what does he have set up for the basement?"

George grinned. "You're going to love this. The answer is...nothing."

"Nothing?" asked Louise. "As in nothing?"

George nodded. "That's right. The basement does have an exit at the other end with a security camera and a light outside the building. You can get out there, but you can't come in. A security guard is on duty in the first-floor lobby from six p.m. until eight a.m. and cameras are set up in the halls on all floors except, ta-dah, the basement. A guard and camera are also set up at the entrance gate, another guard patrols the property on a golf cart, and as he reminded me, despite recent happenings at Whisperwood, this county has a low crime rate and the murderer must have come from outside. I think what he means is that the security force doesn't have to be as vigilant as it would be in a big, crime-ridden city."

"That's what he thinks," muttered Louise.

"Believe it or not," George glanced at Louise, "that's what he thinks."

Fitz looked at his watch. "Classes in the basement end at nine p.m. Most people here, except for the Insomniac Club, are tucked into their apartments by ten. I say we go down to the basement by eight-thirty tonight and hide in an empty classroom. I'll bring my tool belt. We'll probably need it."

"Good," agreed Nancy. "That way we'll avoid the guard in the lobby who will assume everyone is heading to their apartments."

"Sounds okay to me," said George. "We'll only have to hide until a little after nine when everyone should have cleared the basement."

"I refuse to break my wrist this time," Louise added grimly.

They raised their cups. "To the 90s Club," said Nancy.

"I hope we get away with it," grumbled George.

Meet The Insomniacs

Can't sleep? Join other insomniacs for games and conversation every night in the Billiard Room on the second floor or the fifth-floor Library. Open to everyone who finds themselves staring at the walls after bedtime. Bring your warm milk and cookies.

The Whisperwood Breeze,
Newsletter of Whisperwood
Retirement Village

Chapter 10

Nancy and Fitz were back in their apartment and relaxing before dinner. Malone was twining himself around Nancy's feet on his best behavior, obviously ingratiating himself for a big dividend at dinner time. He still spent hours pacing in front of the door and sniffing underneath it into the hall.

"I've got to arrange a play date with Cleo," Nancy said.

Fitz looked up from his book. "Tomorrow for sure."

She heard a knock on the door and opened it to Simon Smythe, the retired jeweler who had helped Nancy defend her pearls against Glinda's shrill denunciation of them as fake, fake, fake. Nancy still heard the words in her mind. "Hello, Simon," she said. "Come in."

He stepped in but hung back as he saw Malone's yellow eyes assessing him. Simon laughed nervously. "He won't eat me, will he?"

Nancy knew Malone wasn't for everybody. "Just a minute. I'll feed him and that will keep him busy." She stepped into the kitchen. Malone followed with loud, demanding meows. To avoid ankle bites, she made quick work of setting down a dish of tuna and refilling his automatic dry cat food feeder.

Meanwhile, Fitz put down his book. "Good to see you," he said. "What brings you to our side of the building?"

Simon hemmed and hawed until Nancy came back and sat down. He was a small, prissy man dressed in a brown suit with a yellow dotted tie. He had stolen jewelry at Whisperwood, but when Nancy confronted him, he had agreed to return it and desist from future thefts. She hadn't checked with Harry on reports of missing jewelry or other items, but most people at Whisperwood who couldn't find something would worry they had misplaced it and were losing their memory, a dread everyone faced at Whisperwood.

"Um, I was in Arabic class this afternoon..." He leaned forward. "You know, I travel a good bit with my business..."

Traveling explained the Arabic class, Nancy guessed. "We were visiting the classrooms down there this afternoon." She glanced at Fitz and added, "We'd heard about the art display and wanted to see it."

Simon didn't buy her story. "But you went all the way down to the end of the hall. I heard there was a door there once. Were you looking for it?"

Fitz laughed. "Nothing left there now. It's just a wall."

"That's right. All the tunnels were filled in." Simon laughed nervously. "Can't get down there anymore. Even that door is blocked up, and I'm told they removed the stairs."

They looked at him. His nervousness increased. He ran a finger under his collar. *What did he want?*

Fitz leaned back and folded his arms. "It was always a dangerous place."

"That's true," Nancy said. "Thank goodness it's all gone now."

"Yes. And the security team is on the alert," Simon said. "Terrible about Alex, though. Who could have murdered him?"

"Let's hope they find the killer soon," Fitz said.

The square mantel clock on the credenza chimed five times. Nancy rose. "We have to go. We're meeting friends for dinner."

Simon got up and smiled. "Ah yes. The 90s Club. We're all grateful to you." He preceded them out the door, and they all strode down the hall to the dining room. Simon left them at the host's desk and continued down the hall.

"What do you suppose he wanted?" whispered Nancy.

"Maybe he doesn't want us messing around in the basement," Fitz said.

"He was fishing for something."

Louise and George were already seated at their usual table fifty-six. They sat on opposite sides of the table and both looked uncomfortable. "Uh oh," Nancy murmured to Fitz as they walked to their table. "George seemed all right with Louise this afternoon, didn't he?"

"I thought so," Fitz agreed.

Tonight, George wore a white dress shirt with gray trousers. No tie. He studied the menu, a serious expression on his face.

Louise greeted Nancy and Fitz, nodded at George's staid outfit, and shrugged. "At least I don't need sunglasses."

"I expected chartreuse tonight," said Nancy to George. "And a bright blue shirt with a pink tie. I miss the colors you usually wear."

"Didn't feel like it," said George, laying aside the menu.

"We've ordered the wine," said Louise. "A French burgundy. They've got pot roast tonight."

"Remember Simon Smythe?" asked Nancy. "He helped me when Glinda insisted my mother's pearls were fake. He showed me how they were a fine set of cultured pearls."

"The squirrelly little man who's a jeweler?" said George, tucking his napkin into his collar. "I bump into him now and then. Reminds me of that old actor Clifton Webb."

Nancy recounted the visit with Simon. "Fitz thinks Simon's worried about the secret door in the basement."

"Can't imagine it," agreed Louise. "What would he be doing in the tunnel?"

The conversation was sparse around the table that evening. The rejected marriage proposal hung in the air and banter between Louise and George was terse and stilted. Adding to the uneasiness was the tension and nervousness they were all feeling about exploring what was behind the secret door. None of them could forget what happened the last time they did this. Dread was on George's face, and Louise rubbed her wrist again and again.

As dessert was served, Nancy said, "Let's go to my apartment until we leave for the basement. I'll make coffee."

"I brought my antihistamines," said George, "in case we get into the tunnel with all that dust. They'll be handy if we end up in Nancy's apartment, too."

No question he'd need them there with the cat dander and dust. Nancy's father had hired a house-keeper during Nancy's growing-up years, so she had no skills in that area. When Fitz moved in, she tried to hire a cleaning service, but none of the staff want-ed to deal with Malone who disapproved of them and unsheathed his claws in resentment at their intrusion.

As the 90s Club approached her apartment, Nancy saw her next-door neighbor, Caroline Richards, in the hall outside Nancy's door, holding a fidgeting Cleo in her arms. She looked at Nancy with relief when she arrived. "Could Cleo visit Malone for a few minutes?" she asked.

This was a bad time for such an interruption, but Malone had also acted fidgety all day. Nancy didn't have the heart to refuse. "Okay," she said.

Caroline walked into Nancy's apartment with Cleo, who jumped out of her arms and ran to Malone.

"Have you met Louise and George?" Nancy asked, introducing them. "They came by after dinner for a little while."

"That's nice," said Caroline. "It's easy to make friends here, isn't it?"

They sat in the living room, watching Malone and the kitten play. Nancy made decaf coffee and brought out cups, sugar, and cream.

"I just heard that someone was killed here," began Caroline. "Do you know anything about it?"

The 90s Club members looked at each other. "We heard about it, too," Nancy said tentatively.

Caroline shuddered. "I thought this would be a safe place to live."

"It is," said Nancy. "The victim was a stranger here."

"I heard he was looking for a trunk," said Caroline. "One of those old-fashioned things. Can't imagine why."

If newcomer Caroline knew about the trunk, thought Nancy, then that must be from the gossip flying around Whisperwood. Glinda had bragged about her singing career in Alaska and proudly displayed the Russian boundary plate on her hall shelf, but she hadn't said much about her brassbound trunk. Nancy knew about it because Glinda had asked Nancy to help move it inside her apartment. It wasn't on display, but neither Alex nor Sterling had kept their interest in the trunk a secret, and notices for help finding it had been posted.

The 90s Club sat in the living room, sipping coffee and making conversation with Caroline while watching Malone and Cleo and surreptitiously glancing at their watches. Caroline seemed oblivious to the restlessness around her. Finally, Louise stood and nodded at Nancy's mantel clock. "It's getting late," she said. "Time to leave." She walked to the door.

Nancy stood, too. "Time for Cleo to go home." She picked up Cleo and handed the kitten to Caroline.

"How about another play date tomorrow?"

Caroline took the kitten reluctantly, obviously willing to stay much longer. Nancy walked her to the door while Fitz drew Malone into the kitchen. Then she stayed at the door until Caroline disappeared inside her apartment.

"Thought she'd never leave," George grumbled. "Louise will meet us downstairs."

Fitz retrieved his tool belt from the closet and inspected it before buckling it around his waist.

"Let's get down to business," Nancy said and put her finger to her lips as they tiptoed past Caroline's door.

Notice to Residents
Quiet Time Begins at Ten P.M.

Please remember to consider your neighbors and keep the volume down on your TV sets and other devices, silence your dogs, and mute your wind chimes after 10 p.m. Everyone needs their beauty sleep. We all appreciate considerate neighbors.

The Whisperwood Breeze,
Newsletter of Whisperwood
Retirement Village

Chapter 11

By ten o'clock at Whisperwood, everyone but the insomniacs were tucked into their apartments. Some showed a light under the door and buzzed with the low tones of a television show. Most were dark. The lights in the hallways were dimmed.

The 90s Club had come down to the basement a few minutes before nine and hidden in a vacant room until the classes in the other rooms let out. They spoke in whispers and did not turn on the lights. Nancy knew the others were as tense and nervous as she felt. The last time they'd gone down into the tunnels, they had encountered a dead body and were almost killed themselves.

This is like going into battle, Nancy thought. We're all afraid. Indeed, George hung back and Louise's face was grim. The basement was soon deserted, as they expected. The lights were automatically turned low, although the display cases for the arts and crafts room were still lighted, adding extra illumination.

They walked to the end of the hall and stood in front of the wall. Fitz examined it on both edges, then looked for seams or cracks. "It's a plywood panel," he said, "but it still has a door," he said. "Someone changed the way it opens, and I'm trying to figure out how it works." He stood back and studied it. "If I can't open it one way, I'll try another." He drew a screwdriver out of the toolbelt and used it on a screw halfway up the door at the edge. He unscrewed it enough to pull on it. The door opened a crack.

"Aha!" he said. The other three clapped softly.

"Someone has been using this door," said Fitz. "They added that screw to keep the door tightly closed. Unscrew it a bit and it serves as a doorknob," said Fitz. "Clever idea." He pulled on the screw and opened the door all the way.

Nancy took out her phone and began taking pictures.

They peered through the doorway into a dark cavernous space, lit by the hall light behind them. Their long shadows leaped across the void to the opposite wall. Stairs reached from the doorway where they stood to the tunnel floor.

Nancy tested the first step. "It feels solid," she said. "I'll bet it's still in use. Let's go down."

George backed away, pushing air with his hands. "Not me. You go. I'll wait here."

"Me, too," said Louise. "My wrist hurts just thinking about it." She held it up.

Nancy nodded sympathetically. "Okay," she said. "Fitz and I will see what's down there and report back."

"Please don't find any dead bodies," Louise added.

Fitz pulled a high-powered flashlight out of his

toolbelt, but a motion light came on as he and Nancy descended the stairs. They stepped onto the stone floor of the tunnel. It felt dry and smelled of dust and mustiness. When they had last climbed down the stairs, they had stepped into a dark tunnel that veered off in both directions with branches to other tunnels along the way. This time, stone walls faced them in every direction, leaving only a large room at the foot of the stairs. Metal shelves and plastic containers lined the walls. Silver bowls and candlesticks gleamed in the light, colorful vases and pottery brightened the walls, and crystal stemware and dishes sparkled on the shelves.

"I feel like we stumbled into Tut's tomb," said Nancy in wonder as she continued to photograph the scene.

"I wonder what's in the boxes," added Fitz. "Gold bars?"

"You okay down there?" called Louise from the head of the stairs.

"Yes. It's just a room. All the tunnels are blocked off," Nancy replied.

Fitz had begun examining the items on the shelves. "Miscellaneous junk, it looks like," he said. "Collections of pottery, ceramics, sculptures..." He moved to another shelf. "Silverware. I think it's sterling. He picked up a box and opened it. "Jewelry. This stuff can't be real." He showed it to Nancy.

She looked closely at several of the pieces but shook her head. "Simon would know."

She walked to a corner of the room and poked behind a pile of boxes.

Then she gasped. "Oh my gosh," she said.

Hidden at the pile's core was Glinda's brassbound trunk.

Fitz was by her side in an instant, shining the light on the trunk. Even though it was tarnished, the brass fittings gleamed.

"Who hid all this stuff down here?" Nancy asked.

Fitz grabbed hold of a handle. "Help me pull it out."

She put the phone in her pocket and grabbed the handle on the other side. They pulled the trunk out of the pile of boxes. It was locked with an old-fashioned padlock that was severely corroded. Fitz grabbed a hammer out of his toolbelt and gave the padlock a severe blow. The lock opened.

Nancy pulled it off, and they raised the lid. Inside was the Russian boundary plaque.

She gaped at it a moment as Fitz peered into the trunk.

"What's going on?" called Louise.

"We found Glinda's trunk and the boundary plaque," Nancy said.

George drew back while Louise stepped forward onto the steps to peer down into the musty, cold chamber. "Someone stole the trunk and the plaque. All this other stuff must be stolen, too." Louise carefully walked down the steps.

Fitz nodded. "The question is, who's the thief?" He was feeling his way around the walls. "I'm just checking to make sure there's not some other door with a way out of here."

"Good idea," said Nancy as she took out her phone. I'm taking pictures of the layout of the room and the items on the shelves."

Finally, Fitz shook his head. 'I can't figure out why someone would hide their stash here, It's way too inconvenient to haul it down the stairs in the first place and then even harder to retrieve it."

Louise tried to pick up the trunk by one of its handles. "This thing is heavy."

"Maybe the thief doesn't have a car," said George, "and couldn't transport everything to some commercial storage company the other side of town where no one would see him."

"And there's too much stuff to store in his apartment," Louise added. "Anyway, someone might see it there."

"People would see him carrying it in the halls, too," said George, "There's a lot here."

"What about fingerprints?" asked Louise.

"I'll get my fingerprinting equipment," Nancy said. "It's not even eleven o'clock yet. I'll go back to my apartment and call Harry. He has to see this. I'll wait for him at the door." She stepped toward the stairs. "We need him in case he knows about this place, and why all these valuable items are stored here."

Louise glanced around. "There could be some legitimate reason, I suppose..."

"In a pig's eye," muttered George. "Anyway, if we get this stuff out of here, where are we going to put it? Not in my place. No, thank you."

"My apartment," said Fitz. "Now that I'm living with Nancy, it's empty. Nobody goes in there."

"Excellent idea," agreed Nancy. "I'm going to get Harry." She proceeded to climb the stairs. "You stay here. I'll bring bags to take as much of this other stuff as we can to Fitz's place."

"Ask Harry to get one of those laundry carts," suggested Louise. "We can put the trunk in that."

"It's too heavy." Fitz said, staring at the trunk with his hands on his hips. "We can't get it up the stairs." He reached for the screwdriver in his tool belt. "I'll have to take it apart."

"Okay." Nancy left Fitz to tackle the trunk while she returned to her apartment by way of the stairs nearest to it. Conscious of the security cameras, she tried to walk as if she had simply visited someone in their apartment and was now returning to her own. Think innocent, she told herself.

It took Harry a few minutes to answer the phone with a groggy, "What is it?"

Nancy explained the situation to Harry's disbelief.

"No way," he exclaimed. "That entire tunnel system is blocked off."

"There's an open section reached by a secret door in the basement," Nancy said.

"What? No, no..." He turned silent. "Well..."

Nancy pounced. "So you did leave an accessible room under the basement."

"Those tunnels are blocked off," Harry said stubbornly. "And we put in a solid wall at the end of the hall."

"That so-called solid wall has a door in it," Nancy said bluntly.

"We did not authorize a door."

"Whatever. There is a door in the wall now." This

was wasting time. "We need you to come here and help us take out the stash that's hidden down there and put it somewhere else."

"But… but...," sputtered Harry. "Can't we do this tomorrow?"

"We need to be secret about this." Nancy tapped her foot impatiently. "We don't know who's responsible, and I think all the items hidden there are stolen." Harry was still young for his job and had had a lot of unusual challenges thrown at him, but he should understand that they needed to work fast.

"Okay," he said grudgingly. "I'm coming right over."

"I'll meet you at the lobby entrance," Nancy said, "but we need to tell the security guards something, so they won't follow us. Until the murderer is caught, we need to keep this secret."

"Tell them anything, the bathroom in your apartment is leaking, whatever." He hung up.

Nancy gathered several tote bags and walked down the hall to the lobby. The security guard looked up from his cell phone. "Couldn't sleep?" he asked.

"Got a leak in my apartment. Called the administrator," She peered at her watch. "Should be here in a few minutes."

"Oh. Okay." The guard returned to studying his phone.

Harry's car squealed to a stop under the portico and he rushed into the lobby. The security guard nodded at Harry as he and Nancy hurried down the hall and then took the back stairs to the basement. Harry opened the door to the laundry room and pulled out a large cart. Nancy took it to the secret door where George and Louise were standing. George peered into the laundry basket. "Might be big enough," he said. "Keep that here to cart things. Fitz is taking off the trunk cover and whatever else he can remove, so we can bring it up in pieces. He says it's heavy."

Nancy pulled a handful of plastic gloves out of a tote. "Put these on, everybody."

"Good," said Louise. "Glad you thought of this. You got the fingerprinting kit?"

Nancy nodded and pulled it out of another tote. I'll go down and see what I can do before the rest of you."

"Oh my gosh," said Harry as he gazed in wonder down the stairs at the tunnel room. "Who would have thought? I gave no authorization for this."

"You haven't seen anything yet," said Fitz. "Look at this." He pulled out of his pocket a glittering array of blue and red stones. "They're either glass or sapphires and rubies, and I don't know why anyone would hide glass. I found them in the holes drilled for the screws that held the trunk together."

"That's why the trunk was so sought after," said Nancy.

"I wonder what else we'll find," Fitz replied as he removed the trunk's cover and handed it to Louise. She carried it up to George.

"Hey," said George. "Let's get a security guard to help."

Nancy and Louise looked at each other. Then Louise said, "No way. We don't know what this is about yet. This is all extremely strange. I say we take the stuff, hide it with Harry's help, document everything we do and take, and find out what's going on."

They left Nancy working with the fingerprinting kit on the trunk, shelves, and several pieces of jewelry, but her efforts were unsuccessful at turning up even a bit of a print. Finally, she looked at the others in resignation. "He must have worn gloves," she said. "I'm not getting anything."

She put the kit away and distributed the tote bags. "Fill them with everything in here and take them up to George to put in the laundry basket."

Harry circled the room muttering, "I can't believe this."

Fitz glanced at him with a lifted eyebrow. "You had no idea...?"

"I knew the crew left a small chamber to save a little on the cost, " said Harry, "but that wall up there was supposedly built to be sturdy."

"Somebody saw a use for this area and outsmarted you," said Fitz, returning to taking apart the trunk.

In an hour, they had emptied the chamber and trooped up the stairs into the basement hall. Fitz secured the secret door. "Nobody would know that door was there," Nancy said, "and it still looks undisturbed."

"I'm going to tell the security chief to put a camera down here and train it at the door," said Harry.

"Don't do that yet." Nancy put her finger to her lips. "Keep it quiet. We don't want to alert the thief that we found his stash because he'll disappear and we'll never catch him."

"I don't know..." Harry said.

"We haven't let you down before," said Louise. "Don't bungle this."

The word "bungle" made Harry flush. "Okay," he said. "I'll trust you."

Because of the laundry cart, they had to take the elevator up to the lobby, but Harry stopped to engage the security guard while the others pushed the cart to Fitz's unused apartment and unloaded it there. Then Nancy took the cart back down to the basement, waving to Harry as she passed.

"We'll get that leak fixed in the morning," Harry said for the guard's benefit. He turned to Nancy. "I'll see you in the morning, too."

Harry was not happy.

Notice to the Residents
Help Keep Small Problems Small

Please report dripping faucets, plumbing leaks, and appliance problems to the receptionist as soon as possible. Simply fill out the form provided, and an experienced handyman will contact you to arrange a time to visit your apartment. He will assess the situation and make necessary repairs before the problem becomes a big one. Thank you.

Harry Doyle,
Administrator

Chapter 12

Despite the late night, Nancy took her place at a card table in the lobby the next morning, setting up her laptop and "Information" sign. The first person to drop by was Caroline Richards, who was concerned about the "late-night shenanigans" that had kept her awake the night before.

"Sounded like someone was moving a cart down the hall," she said accusingly, "and some of the noise came from your apartment."

"The bathroom in my apartment leaked, and I called Harry. He had to bring equipment down the hall," Nancy improvised. "It won't happen again, I'm sure."

"Oh. Okay," said Caroline. "See any signs of that murderer?"

"You don't need to worry about murderers," Nancy said. That was a lie, but Nancy crossed her fingers and hoped the 90s Club would catch the killer soon. "Whisperwood has a competent team of security guards patrolling the building and the grounds."

Caroline shook her head. "Seems like the killer

was too clever for them. What was that young man doing here? Seems like he got what he deserved."

Nancy was surprised at such a harsh assessment. "It was outside the building on the far end of the grounds. The security team has increased surveillance and is doing everything they can to prevent crimes on the campus."

"I hope so," Caroline said. "I moved here for a quiet and safe place." She hung around the table a few minutes longer. Nancy felt Caroline was fishing for more information or more reassurance or more something but what?

Caroline finally left, not entirely satisfied. Nancy had done her best, but she felt uncomfortable at the ease with which the 90s Club had circumvented the security measures at Whisperwood. The stash in the tunnel room indicated that criminal activities were still going on despite the security patrols. The problem is, she thought, that everything here—the place, the people, the activities—seems clean, honest, and open to scrutiny on the surface, but most people at Whisperwood had dark secrets. Even me, Nancy said to herself. And some residents had acquired their wealth in unsavory ways.

The next visitor was a sad-faced woman, crumpled tissue in hand, who sat at Nancy's table, shaking her head. "I think I've been a fool," she said. "My friend Gwen said I should talk to you."

She was one of the younger residents, in her sixties, Nancy guessed, and she looked through blue eyes under blonde curly hair. Her mouth trembled.

"What happened?" asked Nancy.

"I met a man online," she said, "on one of those dating sites, you know."

Nancy knew what was coming. Despite the lectures she had set up at Whisperwood on scams and frauds targeting the elderly, every week brought new victims to her table.

"How much did he take you for?" asked Nancy, cutting to the chase.

"Five hundred dollars."

Nancy breathed easier. One woman's online boyfriend had milked her in installments totaling ten thousand dollars before she got wise. "Don't send him any more money," said Nancy. "Cut him off completely."

"Can I get my money back?" asked the woman.

Nancy shook her head. "It's gone." She recommended a useful website, romancescams.org, to learn more about how she'd been duped to prevent it from ever happening again.

"He seemed like such a nice man," the woman said, still mourning a dream turned nightmare.

Harry dropped by when she left. "I've gotten a couple of complaints about noise in the hall last night," he said.

"Me, too." Nancy shrugged.

"I still think the chief of security should install a camera in that room and the basement hall," he said.

"Wait. Don't do anything yet," Nancy said. "We agreed to hold off on that. She pushed back her chair and stood. "Let's talk in your office."

Harry glanced around the lobby. Bella had ambled in, poured herself a cup of coffee, and now sat in an armchair nearby. "Okay," he said.

Nancy led the way to Harry's office and took a seat. Harry closed the door and sat at his desk. He stroked his chin. "You're right," he finally said. "The guards and most of the staff live in town, too. They're not supposed to talk about their work, but they do."

"The fewer people know about the tunnel room," Nancy said, "the better right now. We need to find out who is responsible, but he thinks he is safe, nobody knows about the room, and he won't go near it if he hears of any security activity in the basement."

Harry tapped a pencil on his desk as he thought. "We can't wait too long. We have to do something."

"The 90s Club is on the job," Nancy said. "You can trust us, but the sheriff has a different agenda."

"He has his eye on the next election," agreed Harry. "I don't trust him, but Whisperwood is a large voting bloc. He has to pay attention to that." He shrugged.

"How is the sheriff doing in his investigation?" asked Nancy, knowing the sheriff had little law enforcement background. After all, his main job was to collect taxes and perform other administrative civic duties. She didn't know what kind of investigative experience Lt. Harmason had. Whisperwood had brought big city problems to this small rural county in West Virginia.

Harry shook his head. "His investigator has been talking to residents and the security staff, but I don't think he's making headway."

"Whisperwood's chief of security is leaving the investigation up to the sheriff's office, too. Barbara and Donald Elmo keep harassing all of them. Of course, they want their grandson's killer caught."

"Most of the articles we took out of the underground room might have been stolen," said Nancy. "Do you have a list of items reported missing here?"

"I'll send you a copy," said Harry. "The problem is that our residents are elderly. They worry they'll be shut up in the Memory Unit, so they don't file a report."

"We'll make a list of all the items we took out of that room," Nancy said. "We might remember seeing a piece in someone's apartment and can ask about it. See if they missed it." Nancy decided not to remind Harry how easily the belongings of recently deceased residents were pilfered in the past before relatives arrived to clean out the apartment.

"We should tell the security team or the investigator what we found," Harry said. His phone rang.

"Not yet," Nancy said, alarmed. In his bumbling way, Harry could tip off the thief. She stood. "Let us continue our investigation first. We know the people here and the setup."

Harry pursed his lips. "All right. I'll give you a week for this. After that, I'm going to the security team."

He picked up the phone and Nancy returned to the information table, nodding at Bella, still sipping coffee and sitting in the armchair like a colorful daffodil.

She got up and took a chair at Nancy's table.

"How can I help you?" asked Nancy.

"I've got a brilliant idea," Bella said. "You'll love it. It's a surefire way to find out who killed Alex Elmo, the poor boy."

"What is that?" Nancy asked, not expecting much.

"We'll hold a séance," Bella said gleefully, "with all the people who knew Alex or Glinda or the Elmos. We're all the main suspects, anyway."

"Probably," Nancy conceded, turning the idea over in her mind. Could such a hackneyed scenario serve any purpose? "But we don't know why he was killed. It may have nothing to do with Glinda or the people she knew."

"Not likely," Bella sniffed. "Getting everyone together for a séance might turn up something interesting, don't you think? Even if Alex's ghost doesn't appear."

"The Elmos might find a séance too painful."

"Oh, pooh. Alex was a misery to his whole family when he was alive," Bella said, waving a hand dismissively."They probably want this investigation cleared up as fast as possible."

They both turned to see Vicki running down the hall toward them.

"Has my sister been telling you about her stupid idea?" she asked Nancy. "Séances went out in the Twenties. Ridiculous idea."

"We've been discussing it," said Nancy. "I'll bring up the suggestion to the 90s Club."

"Don't bother," said Vicki. "I refuse to have us associated with such nonsense."

"It is not nonsense," Bella fumed. "A séance will bring the suspects together so we can watch them."

"Ignore her," said Vicki, tugging on Bella's arm.

As they left with Bella protesting and Vicki pulling her down the hall, Louise showed up in her beekeeping outfit.

"How are all your little employees doing?" Nancy asked.

"Buzzing away," Louise answered, lifting the smoker she carried in one hand. Her netted beekeeping hat was in the other. "Need to take a quick look in the hive, add some medication. This one's getting so large, I'm expecting them to swarm, I'm going to buy a new hive to handle the overpopulation."

"After lunch, drop by my apartment." Nancy saw another resident heading her way. "We need to talk."

Louise waved and went on her way as the other resident, appearing upset and worried, took the seat Bella had vacated.

"How can I help you?" asked Nancy.

Spring Rains Mean Slippery Steps
The security team urges all residents to take care on the walks and steps around Whisperwood to avoid falls and accidents. This safety measure also applies to those of you using mobile scooters and wheelchairs. Speeding is not permitted in the halls or on the walks outside. All of our residents expect and deserve a safe experience at Whisperwood.

The Whisperwood Breeze,
Newsletter of Whisperwood
Retirement Village

Chapter 13

Nancy bought a couple of sandwiches at the Pub and returned to her apartment for lunch. Fitz was reading while Malone prowled back and forth at the door. The cat tried to dodge Nancy and sneak out into the hall, but Nancy shut the door too fast.

Fitz glanced up. "He's been scratching and sniffing at the door all morning."

"He wants to play with Cleo, I guess." Nancy felt sorry for the poor cat and called him into the kitchen for a tuna treat. "I've got lunch."

"Great." Fitz joined her in the kitchen. "George called. Wants to know what to do next."

"I asked Louise to come by after lunch."

"I don't think that's a good idea," Fitz said. Then he put a finger to his lips and wrote on a pad of paper, "I'm worried this place is bugged. Something seems off." He handed it to Nancy.

"Sorry. I forgot," said Nancy as she scribbled on the pad, "We need to list all the items we took from the underground room." She handed the pad back to Fitz and filled glasses with ice and water.

"Good idea," Fitz wrote. "I want to examine

that trunk more closely. It's full of secret places." He walked into the bedroom and returned with a glass jar containing sparkly red, blue, green, and colorless faceted gemstones. Then he wrote, "I'm sure more pieces like these are hidden in the trunk. Where did Glinda get them? Why not hide them in a safety deposit box?"

"Her admirers probably gave them to her," Nancy wrote and then whispered. "She was 'The Singing Canary,' you know."

Fitz laughed. "She might have been involved in dubious activities in Alaska and never knew when she'd have to leave town fast. She wanted to keep her wealth with her."

"From what her sister once told me, that could be true. They grew up in Alaska as poor orphans."

"Sad story." Fitz munched his sandwich thoughtfully.

Someone knocked on the door.

Nancy opened it a crack to see Caroline holding Cleo. Malone twined himself around Nancy's legs and purred. Nancy let Caroline slide through the door. "I have a favor to ask," she said as Cleo scrambled to get out of her arms.

Malone stretched up toward Cleo. "We'll be glad to help," Nancy said.

"May I leave Cleo here for a couple of hours? I need to run into town, and she has been pining at the door. I thought they might like some time together." She let Cleo jump to the floor and go to Malone.

"Of course. Malone has also been pining for her all morning. We have quite a love match here. You go on and do your errands."

For a few minutes after Caroline left, Nancy watched the two cats play but was reassured as she saw how gently Malone treated Cleo when they snuggled together. Amazing, Nancy thought, mesmerized at the change in Malone.

An hour later, they heard another knock, and then Louise walked in. "Hey, you forgot to lock the door. For shame." George followed behind her. "We're here for the meeting," she said.

"I've taken my allergy pills," added George, looking suspiciously at Malone and Cleo. "Cleo back again? We gonna have kittens?"

"Playdate. Malone's friend, and he's neutered," said Nancy. "Glad you're here. We have a job to do." She pulled several small notebooks out of a desk drawer and handed one to each of the others. She motioned for them to go into the hall and held up a sign saying, "Apartment might be bugged. Go to Fitz's place."

His apartment was a short way down the hall. Nancy locked her door behind her, leaving Malone and Cleo playing in her living room.

Fitz's apartment was a disorganized jumble of furniture and boxes, with additional chaos caused by the items from the tunnel storeroom.

"We need to list the items we took from the underground room, Nancy said, "but first you might enjoy hearing about Bella's brilliant plan." She glanced at Fitz and winked.

Louise folded her arms. "Okay. I'm ready," she muttered.

"She thinks we should hold a séance..." Nancy paused as the others groaned, "with everyone who knew Alex, Glinda, or the Elmos."

"Bella's an entertainer like Glinda," George said. "She sees this as an opportunity to play the role of Madam See-All."

"On the positive side," Fitz said, "it would bring the obvious suspects together where they might reveal some hidden motives."

Nancy glanced at him. "That's what I thought, too."

"I guess it might be useful," agreed Louise, "but let's put that on the back burner for now and start listing the jewelry we found that might have been stolen from the residents."

"I don't want anyone to say we're thieves," muttered George.

Nancy looked at him. "I'm sure they were stolen, all right, but not by us."

"Come on, George." Louise poked him with her elbow. "Let's get on with it."

They spent two hours listing the items, including identifying marks, conditions, and any prices indicated. One polished lacquer box was lined with black felt and contained several necklaces, brooches, earrings, and rings. They were all set with diamonds, rubies, sapphires, and other stones. Nancy examined them closely. "The settings are marked as 18-karat gold, sterling silver, or what might be platinum. If that's correct, then I think the stones are genuine."

Fitz spent the time continuing to take apart the trunk. Each time he removed a screw, several glittering stones dropped out of the hole, and he placed those in the jar. After the trunk was dismantled, Fitz took a closer look at the brass and lacquered binding strips.

Nancy heard him whistle. "I say, look at this, Nancy."

She turned to him. "What's up?"

Fitz scratched the black paint off one of the bindings with his screwdriver. Bright gold showed in the scratches. He looked up at Nancy. "I think this strip is gold disguised with a coat of black lacquer. The other bindings are brass."

George turned around. "Say what?"

"Feel how heavy this strip is?" Fitz held up one of the strips and passed it around.

"It's a lot heavier than the other strips," Louise said.

Fitz nodded. He held up the jar of gemstones and rattled it. "The screws held the binding strips in place to keep the trunk together and also plugged deep holes where gemstones were hidden."

George whistled. "That Glinda was a piece of work."

"She must have been very afraid," said Nancy.

"I don't have any idea how to evaluate the stones," said Fitz, "but I'll make a list of what I found and put them in my safety deposit box."

"Wait," said Louise. "Right now we're all witnesses to what we found. We need to give that jar to Harry to put in the Whisperwood safe. We can all sign a paper documenting the contents, so no one can accuse us of stealing or replacing genuine stones with fake ones." She paused a moment, finger tapping her chin. She looked at Nancy. "How do we know the rocks in the jar are genuine?"

"Context," said Fitz. "Why would she hide fakes?"

George nodded. "Anyway, the list is a good idea. Accountability, you know. We need to do that for all the stuff we found."

"I'll collect your lists, put the information on a spreadsheet, and send Harry a copy we can all sign," Nancy said. "Don't tell anyone, and I'll caution Harry, too."

"We now know why there was so much interest in Glinda's trunk," said Louise.

"Only from Sterling Cooper and Alex Elmo. Barbara and Don Elmo weren't interested. They didn't know." Nancy's eyes roved over the lists. "Neither did Cary and Clark. How did Sterling and Alex find out about Glinda's secret stash?"

"We'll need three separate categories," said Fitz, rubbing his chin. "one for the pebbles in the jar; one for the other jewelry we found; and one for the keepsakes, antiques, and other items."

Nancy gestured to the colorful array of jewelry and artifacts. "Do you recognize anything familiar? An item you might have seen in someone's apartment?"

"Glinda was dead way before that tunnel room was used to stash this stuff, so we have another thief here," said Louise.

Nancy suddenly laughed. "I know where I've seen that lamp and those Lenox china swans."

"Where?" asked Louise. "That ought to tell us who they belonged to."

Nancy shook her head. "Helen Strassberg's apartment. She died several months ago. Her relatives should have them."

Fitz scratched his chin and picked up one of the china swans. "The thief probably got into the apartment and took what he wanted before the relatives could claim it."

"That used to happen regularly," said Nancy. "with the previous administration."

They stood silent a moment remembering.

"Maybe the thief planned to sell everything online. We should look for someone who does that," said George.

Nancy scanned the room. "The thief can't be a newcomer. He or she has to be someone who knew about the tunnels and what happened a year ago."

"Not necessarily," said Fitz. "You know how people talk here."

Louise nodded. "We found out who the thieves were last year, and all the stolen items were returned. This stuff was taken since then."

"And the thieves we caught are dead or in prison," said Nancy. "Only Simon is still here, but he promised to desist."

George frowned. "Once a thief, always a thief."

Fitz took a chair and began putting the trunk together again but without the gemstones.

"The plot thickens," he said. "We have a thief as well as a murderer to find, and we don't know if they are one person or two or more."

"He had to be very strong to have hauled that trunk down to the tunnel room," added Louise, "or he hired someone and that could be a weak link."

"But who could he hire to do that work?" asked

George. "How could he be sure they wouldn't blab about it?"

"Doesn't have to be a resident," Nancy said. "Could have been someone on staff or a visitor."

Woodworking Shop Seeks Projects

Whisperwood's woodworkers and carpenters are seeking new projects so if you have a broken chair, table, or other furniture that needs repair, bring it to the Woodworking Shop, basement level, between ten a.m. and noon on Mondays, Wednesdays, and Fridays.

They will also accept any wooden furniture or other pieces of maple, oak, or other fine wood for reworking.

Drop by the shop and see what other projects these handy crafters are working on.

If you have questions or want to learn more about this project, contact Andy Wilson, 304/555-9334.

The Whisperwood Breeze,
Newsletter of Whisperwood
Retirement Village

Chapter 14

Later that afternoon, Nancy gave the spreadsheet, the jewelry, and the jar of gemstones to Harry, cautioning him to keep them secretly in the safe for the time being. Fortunately, he respected Nancy and her past successes at Whisperwood and so he agreed.

"We brought up a lot of other items, too," Nancy added, "like candelabras, small antiques, bric-a-brac that probably don't have much value but might also have been stolen from the residents. They're in Fitz's apartment. We'll inventory them later."

Harry nodded thoughtfully. "So what we have are loose gems that Glinda got from someplace, jewelry that might have been stolen from the residents, and bigger items that may also have been stolen."

"That's right," Nancy said. "The jewelry and loose stones are inventoried and to be put in your safe. The bigger pieces, antiques and what-not, are in Fitz's apartment."

Harry shook his head. "This is a nightmare."

"Give me the residents' reports of missing items, and I'll compare them to the lists of jewelry and other items we found. We'll return the objects to the proper owners when we're through investigating," she said. "By the way, does Whisperwood have a custodian who is especially strong?"

"Peter Armstrong," Harry replied absentmindedly as he glanced over the list. "A real handyman. Helped a lot of residents with odd jobs."

"I'd like to speak with him," Nancy said.

Harry shook his head. "Can't. He died several months ago."

"He's dead?" Nancy felt goosebumps. "How?"

Harry looked at her. "Odd thing. Seems he was allergic to peanuts and mistakenly ate cookies made with them. Died of shock."

How convenient, Nancy thought.

Harry shivered. "Good worker, too. People here loved him."

"I remember him," said Nancy, "but I thought he'd moved away."

Her next visit was to Simon Smythe, the jeweler who had helped her appraise her pearls when Glinda had cruelly dismissed them as fake. He had also turned out to be a jewel thief, Nancy learned later, but he had agreed to stop and return the stolen items if she would not report him to the police. They struck this uneasy bargain, which gave Nancy a resource for help in the specialized area of expensive jewelry. It also placed him high on the list of suspects.

Simon opened the door. He seemed surprised. "Nancy! What brings you here?" Behind him, sitting in the living room, was Sterling Cooper. He rose halfway off the couch and bowed to her.

"You two know each other?" Nancy asked, covering her surprise. "He says he came from Alaska and was Glinda's ex-husband."

Sterling looked at her. "I was, and we remained friends."

"And I had known her a long time," Simon said smoothly. "We were talking about old times back in Alaska. I was a fan of Glinda's. She had a lovely voice." He leaned toward Nancy as if he were imparting a secret. "Everyone called her the 'Singing Canary,' you know."

Nancy almost laughed. "Yes, I know," she said. "May I join you?"

Simon waved her in and she took the nearest armchair. "Would you like a cup of coffee?" he asked.

"Thank you." A plate of cheese and crackers lay on the coffee table.

"Did you know Glinda well?" asked Sterling.

"Well enough," said Nancy. "And I've talked with her two sons."

He laughed. "By the time we met, the boys were in their teens. Hellions they were, too." He winked at her.

"Did you work with Glinda on the stage?"

"I was her manager. Set her up with gigs all over Alaska, western Canada, and Washington State." Sterling laughed. "My Glinda entertained those worn-out losers until they spent all their money and went home."

"She must have been quite successful," Nancy said. "How did you meet Simon?"

Sterling glanced at Simon. "I don't rightly remember."

"Long time ago. In my early days," said Simon. "I

spent a couple of years prospecting in Alaska for the hell of it before I found out it was too hard a way to earn a living."

Nancy couldn't imagine Simon in such a rough occupation. Another dimension to the man. She would have thought he was more suited to tea parties.

Sterling picked up his coffee. "I was shocked, I tell you, when I saw Simon here in the hall. Shocked. It's a wonder I remembered what he looked like. There's someone else here I used to know back in the theater business, too."

"Who is that?" asked Nancy, amazed at the widening circle of Glinda's acquaintances who had found their way to Whisperwood. Could they have been drawn by her wealth or fame? It certainly couldn't have been her winning personality.

"I'm trying to remember her name," drawled Sterling thoughtfully. "It'll come to me and I'll let you know."

"What did she look like?" asked Nancy.

He shrugged. "Old. Like any other woman in this place."

"I see. Beautiful, you mean. Any luck finding Glinda's trunk?" asked Nancy. "Did you check with Cary or Clark?"

"Cary and Teresa took it out of the apartment," said Simon with a warning look at Sterling, "but since then, it has disappeared."

Nancy set her cup down and said casually, "Maybe they put it in the dumpster."

Sterling looked at her in horror. "Surely not. They wouldn't do that, would they, Simon?"

Simon shrugged. "It was just an old footlocker, gussied up with brass strips so she could call it a steamer trunk. Not very valuable."

"Not valuable!" Sterling shrieked. "It was an antique, probably worth a couple of thousand dollars. That trunk should belong to me."

"I don't think so," Simon said coldly.

"If you do find the trunk," Nancy said, "would you let me know? I'm interested."

Simon frowned at her. "I'm sure it had nothing to do with Alex's murder."

Sterling shook his head. "Not good. Not at all what I expected, and now I'm scared to leave my room. A murder!" He eyed Nancy. "Not even sure about you, but I wasn't getting anywhere staying in the house and desperate to get out."

"We're all nervous about the murders," Nancy said. "Whisperwood is supposed to be safe."

Simon looked at Sterling. "Why don't you leave?" he asked. "No reason for you to stick around."

"I've got business here," snapped Sterling. "And I want that trunk. It's mine." Sterling took another sip of the whiskey and sat back to look at the glass fondly.

"How long do you plan to stay?" Nancy asked.

"Don't know," Sterling said. "I'm real upset about what's been going on."

Nancy shrugged. "You and Alex showed up here at the same time and both of you were asking about Glinda's trunk. How did that happen?"

"No big deal," Sterling said. "It took months before news of Glinda's death got around. Then Alex got out of jail. He came around to my place, asking for a handout. He said I owed him 'cause of his great aunt Glinda. He thought I was rolling in the dough she made. Hah!"

"Why would he think that?" asked Nancy.

"When we was married, I worked hard, but she wouldn't let me see a dime. She kept it all and doled out to me cigarette change. She was making good money, too, but she was tighter than rock in a glacier." He pulled a pack of cigarettes out of his pocket.

Simon frowned. "Please. Not in here. Go outside."

Sterling put the unlit cigarette in his mouth. "I ain't smoking," he told Simon. He turned to Nancy. "What did she do with it all? The more I thought about it, the more I decided she must have hidden her money in that steamer trunk, which, I'll have you know, belonged to me. Handed down in my family. I gave it to her, but now I want it back."

"Baloney," said Simon.

Sterling ignored him. "I wrote Barbara, asking if I could have it back for sentimental reasons, you know, but she didn't remember anything about it. Not even Cary or Clark knew where it was. They all thought it was worthless, but I looked up trunks like hers on eBay and found one on auction for $2,000 or more. It was worth something, all right, just the trunk."

"So you decided to come here to find it," said Nancy.

"Yep," said Sterling. "And Alex must have had the same idea, because he came here, too, but it belongs to me and my family."

"Nobody seems to know where it is," said Nancy.

"Somebody has it," said Sterling after a long sip

of whiskey. "Mark my words. They've got it hidden in their apartment. They might already have found Glinda's money." He peered at Nancy. "You watch. Somebody will show up rich and say they won the lottery. Then you'll have your murderer." He took another sip. "And it won't be me."

Nancy left. With Simon's connection to Glinda's past and his own history of stealing at Whisperwood, he became a suspect, too. She couldn't ask him about the jewelry and the gemstones and expect the truth.

***

As usual, the 90s Club met at table fifty-six for dinner. The manager took their wine requests, and the server stood by, pen and pad in hand, for their food orders. The four amateur detectives gave them their selections, sat back, and relaxed.

George fingered his napkin. "With what we've got in Fitz's apartment," he said, "we're probably sitting on a powder keg. The sheriff would arrest us for sure if he found out."

"I gave Harry a copy of the spreadsheet," Nancy said, "but we've got to keep quiet about what we're doing with what we found. Then I went to Simon Smythe's apartment to talk with him."

"The jeweler?" said George. "What's he got to do with anything?"

"I think he is involved somehow, but get this." Nancy paused for dramatic effect. "Sterling Cooper was there."

"Why would he be visiting Simon?" Louise asked.

"He said they'd known each other for years." Nancy unrolled her napkin and placed it in her lap.

"You remember Sterling says he's Glinda's ex-husband and her manager."

George sneezed and took out a tissue. "Allergies," he said, blowing his nose. "So what? This doesn't get us anywhere."

"I don't think Simon knows what's hidden in the trunk," said Nancy, "and Sterling hasn't been here long enough to have stolen the items we found in the basement. Thievery seems more like Simon's work."

"Scrawny little Simon?" scoffed Louise. "I can't see him as a killer."

They stopped talking as the manager brought their wine, a *pinot noir* this time, poured it into their glasses, and left.

"One other thing," Nancy said. "Sterling says he has seen someone here that he knew in Alaska."

"Another one?" scoffed Louise in disbelief. "Is anyone left in Alaska? We've got Barbara and Don, Sterling, Simon... Who is it this time?"

"He couldn't remember her name," Nancy said. "Could have been Barbara."

"All right. I'll believe it when I see it," said Louise. "Meanwhile, we have another problem before us. Ongoing." She raised her glass in Nancy's direction. "Your wedding."

"We told you we're waiting until we clear up Alex's murder," said Nancy. "And we don't want a shower or any fuss." She glanced at George who sat back thoughtfully, his finger tapping the glass of wine.

"This is a big deal," said Louise.

"You'll get the first invitation," Fitz put in.

"And sit at the head table," added Nancy.

Louise glared at her. "Okay, but don't put it off too long."

Problems? Concerns?
Need Handyman?

Whisperwood offers residents several services to help make their lives happier and more comfortable.

Feeling sad? Depressed? Worried? Talk it over with our clinical psychologist, Mary Barker, or our social worker, Jon McKenzie. 304-555-9607.

Need help dealing with consumer fraud or scams? Talk to Nancy Dickenson who is available at the lobby information table on Tuesday and Thursday mornings.

Need minor repairs or help in your apartment? Call our new handyman, Andy Yoho, at 304-555-9608 or submit your request to Ashley at the reception desk.

The Whisperwood Breeze,
Newsletter of Whisperwood
Retirement Village

Chapter 15

Vicki and Bella, the two sisters, confronted the 90s Club members as they left the dining room.

"How is the case coming along?" asked Bella, smiling especially at George. She took his arm as they walked toward the elevator.

George blushed. "We're close to solving it," he said with an apologetic look at Nancy.

"Wonderful!" Bella gushed. "We're hot on the trail, too. None of us will feel safe until the killer is caught. We're doing our part in the investigation."

Nancy cringed. Bella had no idea how dangerous that could be.

Vicki edged out Louise and Nancy to take George's other side. "We'll walk along with you while you tell us all about your day."

Louise glanced at Nancy with a lifted eyebrow. "George is putty in their hands," she whispered to Nancy.

"I'm afraid so," Nancy replied, but she was worried. Would George soothe his bruised ego by blabbing everything to those two adoring females? She couldn't see any way to stop the two sisters from fawning over

George, and she didn't think he was savvy enough to understand their motives, which were obvious enough to the rest of them.

Louise looked at them with disgust on her face.

Fitz spoke up. "Ladies," he said, "we appreciate your interest, but none of us can talk about our investigations. They are ongoing and quite delicate since they involve the residents here, so I'm sure you can understand our need for complete secrecy. We'd appreciate it if you would not ask any questions of us."

Thank goodness for Fitz, Nancy thought. George seemed affronted by Fitz taking control with such a firm stance, but she felt relieved.

"Of course," said Vicki. "We only want to help."

"I'm a people person," Bella said. "My intuitions about the people here could be useful to you. I'll be keeping my eyes and ears open for clues to identify the killer. This investigation is perfect for my skills."

"What planet does she live on?" muttered Louise to Nancy.

"In fact," Bella paused dramatically, "I've recognized one new person here that you ought to be careful around. I'm keeping my eye on her."

"Who is that?" asked Louise.

Bella shook her head. "Never mind. I'm pursuing this on my own."

"Don't put yourselves in danger," cautioned Nancy. "Stay out of it."

"I do think all of you should stay out of it," said Vicki. "Leave it to the trained professionals. The sheriff's office is on the job, and it's a dangerous one."

Fitz took Nancy's arm and waved at them. "All

right," he said. "Have a good night. We'll see everyone tomorrow."

***

Fitz and Nancy had just finished breakfast when
Malone's ears perked up, and they heard a loud knock
on the door. Nancy glanced at the clock. Nine a.m.
Early for a visitor at Whisperwood. Fitz picked up
Malone and closed him in the bedroom. With his pal
Cleo tantalizingly close next door, Malone was always trying to escape these days. Closing him in the
bedroom did not mean he wouldn't make loud complaints, but that was better than chasing him down the
hall or bandaging any wounds he might inflict on visitors.

Nancy opened the door, and Barbara and Don
Elmo barged in past Nancy.

"We need to talk to you," Barbara said. She looked
angry.

"Have a seat," said Fitz with a glance at Nancy.

"Would you like tea?" asked Nancy.

"Nothing, thank you." Barbara sat on the couch
with Don beside her.

"How can we help you?" Nancy asked, sitting in
an armchair.

"Nobody knows where Glinda's brassbound trunk
is," Barbara began.

Don leaned forward, his elbows on his knees.
"We own that trunk now," he said. "Someone stole it
from us."

Barbara's eyes sparked fire. "Maybe that no-good
ex-husband of hers. Manager, my foot."

Nancy stoked the flame. "He seems to think it belongs to him."

"He has no claim to it whatsoever," Barbara said. "It's ours."

"What about Glinda's sons?" Fitz asked. "They should be the rightful heirs."

"They refused it. We heard you've found it," added Don. "We're here to get it back."

"Where did you hear that?" Nancy knew Louise, George, and Fitz would not have talked about it. Neither would Harry.

"Everybody's saying it," insisted Barbara.

"First we've heard about it," said Fitz. "We thought you'd thrown the trunk out."

"We just put it aside," said Don.

"We don't have the trunk," Nancy said firmly because they did not have it. It was not in their apartment. The Elmos must have decided that since Alex and Sterling both claimed the trunk, it must be worth something. They wanted whatever it was.

Fitz stood. "I'm sorry, but we can't help you."

Barbara took the hint. She rose and walked toward the door. Don followed. "That trunk belongs to us," she said. "It was my late sister's and now it's mine."

"We hear you." Nancy watched them amble down the hall, and then closed the door behind them. She turned back to Fitz.

"That was interesting," she said. "A lot of people are suddenly claiming that trunk. And we've found out why."

Fitz let Malone out of the bedroom, and Nancy called Caroline, offering to watch Cleo for a while.

"Thank you, thank you," gushed Caroline. "Cleo

is so restless, she is driving me crazy. I'm afraid to leave her alone when she's like this. She'll rip everything to shreds, and I've got to make a trip to town."

"Bring her over when you're ready," Nancy said, also pleased to give Malone and Cleo time to play with each other.

Notice to the Residents
Update from the Administrator

Because of the circumstances surrounding the recent death on the grounds of Whisperwood, our Security Team has increased the number of guards patrolling the grounds and the building. Strangers to Whisperwood will be identified and removed unless they can prove a legitimate reason to be here. We also ask that you refrain from talking about the incident. Such gossip will only result in mistaken rumors that exaggerate or falsify the actual circumstances.

Please be assured that you have no reason to worry. The victim was a stranger to Whisperwood.

Harry Doyle, Administrator

Chapter 16

Later that morning, Nancy left Fitz in charge of the cats and met Louise in the lobby on the way out for a walk. "Good morning," Nancy said.

"What's good about it?" Louise practically snarled. Her attitude was a bit more confrontational than her usual morning grumpiness.

"What's wrong?" asked Nancy.

"George can do what he wants," fumed Louise, "but how he can put up with those two simpering females is beyond me."

"Oh," said Nancy. She agreed, but didn't want to comment. Instead, she changed the subject. "Do you suppose Bella recognized someone from the past who recently moved here?"

"Who cares? Probably some looney she might have known that has no relevance to our case." Louise was still irritated. "He went with them into town. They invited him to go shopping. Shopping!" Words couldn't describe Louise's contempt. "And he went." Louise snorted. "Unbelievable."

Rather than pour oil on the fire, Nancy again

changed the subject. "We had visitors this morning," she said. "Barbara and Don Elmo."

"Really? What did they want?" Louise followed Nancy out the lobby door, down the drive, and onto the garden path.

"They laid claim to Glinda's trunk. She said everybody knew we'd found it."

"No way," said Louise. "I didn't tell anyone. Of course, now that George is under the spell of those two harridans, he could have told them anything. Anyway, the Elmos were lying. They've decided that since Alex and Sterling wanted it, there must be something valuable about it. Now they want it too."

"Keep your voice down, Louise," Nancy cautioned as she led the way to the garden and the new path under construction. The day was warm, and many residents had opened their windows.

Louise glanced behind her. "No one else is about."

"But you never know. I was thinking about what Fitz found."

"You mean the...?"

"Yes. Where did Glinda get them?"

"I thought maybe she smuggled them in from somewhere on her travels."

"I didn't see a passport anywhere," said Nancy. "She never said anything about being out of the country. Her son said she was xenophobic."

"Not smuggled then." Louise pushed branches aside with her cane.

"Hold onto my arm." Nancy held it out. "Entertainers live precariously, and she was raising two boys. Kids are expensive."

"Maybe she invested in those gemstones and hid them for security," said Louise. "But did she steal them or buy them?"

"That's the question. We don't know."

They were now in the county park area. A stream cascaded down a slope nearby, and the woods bordering Whisperwood's land had opened up into a vista of mountains. "Beautiful," breathed Nancy.

"Whisperwood prevailed against the soul-dead forces that wanted to destroy this beautiful place with a quarry, and now the county has a public park all of us can enjoy," said Louise with satisfaction. She savored the view with her hands on her hips.

"Glinda might have bought the loose gemstones as an investment, probably one or two at a time. They could also have come from thieves who removed them from stolen jewelry and sold them to her," Nancy mused aloud. "The set pieces—rings, bracelets, necklaces, etc., were probably stolen from the residents or elsewhere."

She turned to Louise. "Did you recognize any of the set pieces?"

"I'm not into jewelry, so I didn't pay much attention." Louise threw a pebble into the stream. "But I did see the false bottom Fitz pulled out of the trunk."

"What false bottom?"

"You were too busy itemizing the other stolen items."

Nancy held up her hand as she looked around. "We're talking too loud," she whispered to Louise. "Listen."

A slight breeze rustled the leaves around them,

but the birds had stopped singing. A bush shook and then was still. An unnatural quietness surrounded them. "Someone is hiding behind the shrubbery," Nancy whispered.

Louise glanced at her wrist. "Let's go back," she said.

They turned and increased their pace until they were back on Whisperwood grounds near the garden where several residents were working.

Louise breathed a sigh of relief. "Glad to be back in civilization. Now what were we talking about?"

"The false bottom in the trunk, " Nancy said.

"It was filled with jewelry."

"Wouldn't loose jewelry rattle around?" asked Nancy.

"Not if it was wrapped in folds of loose cotton batting. That fake bottom was about an inch deep. Fitz wouldn't have spotted it if he hadn't taken the trunk apart."

"We need to check those pieces against a database of stolen jewelry online." Nancy wanted to run back to the building and take another look at the pieces of the trunk, but Louise wanted to see what was blooming in the garden. Nancy slowed down.

"Fitz kept the jewelry wrapped up in the cloth, but he dropped the loose gemstones into a jar," Louise reminded her.

"He gave all of it to Harry to put in the safe," Nancy said, "along with the other jewelry we found."

"Which Glinda probably stole from the residents," said Louise.

Back inside the building, they poked their heads

into Harry's office. "Had a chance to check the lists?" asked Nancy.

Harry moaned and shook his head. "I am up to my ears in work." He looked up at them. "They're all safe, though."

"Why don't I check them," said Nancy. "Give me a copy of the list of lost items, and I'll compare the list with what we've found, which is in a spreadsheet on my computer. I can do that job this afternoon with Louise."

Harry brightened. "Good idea."

"There's a bag of jewelry in the safe that I haven't itemized," said Nancy. "I'd like to retrieve it."

"As long as you sign a receipt," said Harry.

"I'll wait in the lobby." Louise turned to leave. "I need to sit down."

Harry rummaged through the pile of papers on his desk and retrieved a folder. "These are the descriptions of lost jewelry furnished by the residents. They should give you enough information to identify any that resemble the pieces you found." He walked back to the safe, opened it, and brought out the bag of jewelry she requested. He placed them in a cardboard box and handed it to Nancy. "Need you to sign a receipt for all this," he said.

Nancy signed the receipt, took the box out of the office, and hid it in her apartment. Then she returned to help Louise get out of the soft encompassing armchair.

"Feels like that chair is grabbing at me," grumbled Louise. "Keeping me down."

They walked to the Pub for lunch. Sterling and

Simon were both at the bar. "Beer for me. Heineken," Sterling told the server.

"A *chenin blanc* for me," said Simon.

They took their drinks to the table where Nancy and Louise had seated themselves. "May we join you?" Sterling asked, turning on the charm.

"Of course," said Nancy. Louise grumbled an assent.

"How is the murder investigation proceeding?" asked Sterling.

"How would we know?" Louise said belligerently with arms folded.

Sterling glanced at Simon. "I understood you were helping the authorities."

"You've solved the other crimes here," Simon added. "Until that murder is solved, none of us will feel safe."

"One of us will," Louise said.

"Who?" asked Sterling.

"The murderer." On that note, the server appeared. Louise ordered her usual BLT and iced tea. Nancy did the same as she studied Simon and Sterling.

She noticed both men seemed at ease. Sterling had arrived only a few days before to claim the trunk he insisted was rightfully his. He would not know about the tunnel room or how to access it. No one but the thief and the 90s Club knew the room existed.

Simon could have known about it, Nancy thought. He could have chosen it as the ideal place to hide his stolen goods. He also might have taken the trunk from wherever Glinda's son or the Elmos had put it and hidden it in the tunnel room, too.

The Elmos could have belatedly learned the trunk was valuable from Alex or Sterling. If they were responsible for the hidden tunnel room, then their performance in Nancy's apartment could have been meant to throw the 90s Club off the scent.

None of the suspects seemed rattled or upset, which they would have been if they had gone to the basement room and found their stash missing. That could mean they were innocent or hadn't yet discovered that the room had been cleared.

"Have you found Glinda's trunk yet?" asked Nancy innocently.

"No, but make no mistake. That trunk belongs to me, no matter what the Elmos say." He nodded at Simon. "Simon here is helping me look for it. He knows this place better than I do."

"It's a valuable antique," Simon said smoothly, "but the Elmos probably scrapped it. Now that they've heard it might be valuable, they want to get in on the gravy train."

"If you run into it anywhere during your investigation," said Sterling, "I hope you'll tell us so I can claim it. It is rightfully mine.'"

Nancy shrugged. "I guess there would be some legal way to handle it. I would leave it up to Harry and the lawyers."

"We'll continue hunting for it then," Sterling said. "I don't trust lawyers."

And Nancy didn't trust either of these men. Simon said the trunk was valuable, but she knew it was battered and in poor condition. From what she understood about antiques and collectibles, the condition of the piece was important.

Simon ought to know that, Nancy thought, so why is he interested? At least Sterling claimed sentimental reasons, and the Elmos want it because the others do.

But whoever hid it in the basement apparently had no idea of its true value.

Maybe Not *Antiques Roadshow* But Close

Most of us have some antique, collectible, or vintage item that we've kept for years or inherited. Here's a chance to ask that question you've been wondering about: How much is it worth? Life Enrichment Director Violet Velois has arranged with antiques appraiser Wallace Pierson to spend Saturday, June 11, at Whisperwood to appraise your precious item. You must sign up with Ashley at the Reception Desk by Wednesday, June 8. Space is limited, so hurry! Everyone is invited to attend to watch. Who doesn't like the *Antiques Roadshow*?

The Whisperwood Breeze,
Newsletter of the Whisperwood
Retirement Village

Chapter 17

Nancy and Louise finished their lunch and left Simon and Sterling still drinking in the Pub. As they crossed the lobby, Violet Velois hailed them. "I'm glad to run into you," she said. "Would you mind stepping into my office for a few minutes? I'd like your opinion."

Nancy was pleased to be asked. They seated themselves in Violet's office as she sat behind the desk.

"I'd like you to go over this interest survey," Violet said. "It would help me find out what kind of programs the residents here would like." She handed each of them a sheet of paper.

Louise jumped in. "More on environmental issues."

Violet made a note. "Perhaps you could take these home and return them later after you've had time to think about the questions." She smiled at them. "I'd also like to know about people with special interests who live here and might like to demonstrate their knowledge and skill in a presentation.

"Like what?" asked Louise.

Violet seemed amused. "Talks about travels to exotic places interest people," she said. "Arts and crafts. What about jewelry? Do we have any jewelers who might talk about how to buy a diamond, say, or pearls?"

Nancy wondered at Violet's amused expression. Were her questions innocent or was she fishing?

Louise grinned at Nancy. "Tell her about Simon Smythe," she said. "Didn't he help you with your pearls?"

"Simon Smythe?" said Violet, writing down the name. "He's a jeweler and he lives here? I'll talk to him."

"How long have you been doing this kind of work?" asked Nancy. "I understand you're an entertainer, too?"

"That's right," Violet said blandly. "I sang with various bands but didn't like being on the road. This way I can keep up with the entertainment world without the travel and contribute a few concerts as well."

"Where did you work before here?" asked Louise.

"Checking my credentials?" Violet smiled. "This is my first job in this capacity, but I do have a lot of experience and contacts in the entertainment world," Violet said.

Uh oh, thought Nancy. How much had Harry vetted this woman? Why was she hired for such an important job with no experience?

Louise glanced at her watch. "I've got to go," she said.

Violet stood. "So nice to speak with both of you. Take the survey along, look over the questions, add any comments, suggestions, or corrections you'd like, and return them to me. Should be a snap."

"We will," said Nancy. "Glad to chat with you."

Nancy perused the survey as they walked back to her apartment. Malone was sleeping against the front door and slid across the oak floor when Nancy opened it. He was ready to spring out, but Louise blocked his way. He stalked off to the bedroom, seriously displeased.

Fitz lay on the couch, reading.

"How did it go?" Nancy asked.

"The cats?" He sat up. "We may end up adopting Cleo just to keep Malone happy. Those two belong together."

"I guess Malone needs a sidekick."

At her desk, Nancy opened the laptop and then the spreadsheet listing the objects discovered in the tunnel room. Louise began reading from Harry's file of items reported lost or stolen by the resdients. The going was slow since Harry's list was not on a spreadsheet and couldn't be sorted. How items were described also varied from Harry's list to Nancy's so they couldn't be sure if an object on one list was the same as an item on the second.

Louise threw down her list in disgust. "There's got to be a better way."

"We do have a couple of items that seem to be on both lists," Nancy said, also feeling stifled by the boredom. "This does seem to be a waste of time. Let's quit this, and I'll continue working on my own later. We need a new system. Meanwhile, I'll go to Fitz's apartment, inventory all the other items, and photograph them to show to the people here who reported a nissing item that matches one on our list."

"In that case, I'm going to check on my bee hives." Louise set the folder on Nancy's desk and headed to the door.

"See you at dinner," Nancy called out as she began a new spreadsheet of the jewelry discovered under the fake bottom of the trunk.

***

As Nancy and Fitz walked to the dining room that evening, Harry confronted them in the hall. "Come to my office, please," he said with a stormy expression and abruptly turned to head for the executive suite.

Nancy looked at Fitz. "What have we done now?" she whispered.

"Doesn't look good," he said.

They followed Harry into his office, and he shut the door behind them. "What do you know about Sterling Cooper?" he asked.

"Why?" Nancy asked, astonished at the question. "He claims to be Glinda's ex."

"Another person from Alaska," added Fitz. "Managed Glinda's performances. What's wrong?"

"He was murdered this afternoon on a back street in town." Harry balled his fist and slammed it on the desk. "Shot dead. Why is this happening to me?"

Nancy gaped at him. "Sterling was killed?"

Harry said through his teeth. "That's what I said. At least it wasn't here, but we all know it was connected to Glinda."

"He reminded me of a lanky cowboy," Nancy said, feeling surprisingly sad for the loss of a man she hadn't liked very much, one who seemed to have achieved so little and yet still hoped for riches.

"He knew something," said Fitz, "that would lead to the killer."

"Obviously," repeated Harry. "But what? He didn't even live here."

"He and Simon seemed to be friends. I saw them together several times," Nancy said. What had Sterling said? Something about seeing someone here he had known in Alaska. But he couldn't remember her name. It was a woman. Bella? Vicki? Violet? Violet had been an entertainer and knew of Glinda.

"Protect yourselves," said Harry. "Stick together. I don't want to lose you, too. That would be the end of Whisperwood."

Nancy and Fitz filed out, sobered and sad. And puzzled. They walked to the dining room to meet George and Louise, but when they took their places at table fifty-six, only Louise was there waiting for them. The server handed them menus, filled the water glasses, and left to find the manager to take their wine orders as usual.

"Where's George?" asked Fitz.

"He defected," Louise muttered, head buried in the menu. "Guy can't take no for an answer."

Nancy surveyed the dining room. "I see him. He's with the two sisters. He's not looking our way."

"What happened?" asked Fitz. "We need him."

Louise laid her menu aside. "If you must know," she said with a sigh, "George is angry with me."

Fitz looked across the dining room and waved at George who seemed intent on ignoring them. "But why? What did you do to him?"

"Said 'No.' He wants me to marry him." Louise folded her arms on the table. "He asked me again a short while ago. And I ain't gonna do it. I was married once. That's enough." She suddenly realized what she'd said. "Oh. Sorry. I meant that's enough for me. Anyone can see you two are made for each other."

Nancy also looked across the dining room at George, sitting with the two sisters, a smug look on his face. They were fawning on him, stoking his ego, and the three of them laughed and giggled as if they were all having a gay ol' time. "Phony," she said. "He'll get tired of it."

"I hope so." Fitz perused the menu.

"So do I," Louise said in a small voice.

The manager dropped by, and the three of them ordered *cabernet sauvignon.*

"Did you hear Sterling Cooper was found dead in town?" asked Nancy.

"What?" said Louise. "Another murder?"

"Must be connected to the lost trunk," noted Fitz.

Nancy nodded. "I'm trying to decide what we should do with the loose stones and jewelry we found."

"Take it all to the police," Louise suggested. "Two murders are two too many."

"I agree," said Fitz, glancing at Nancy. That's what we should do."

"I would also agree," Nancy said, "and I've thought a lot about this. The killer might have hidden the trunk and other stuff, but maybe not. That solution would be an easy answer for Harmason, true or not, and cut off further investigation. The thief and the murderer could be two different persons. I say let's find out what we can, track down the thief, and then see where we are before going to Whisperwood's security team or the sheriff."

"Harry would prefer the security team handle that to keep this problem amongst ourselves," Louise commented, "to protect Whisperwood's reputation."

"All right," said Fitz, "but let's give ourselves a deadline, say three days, and then turn everything over to the security team."

"That sounds reasonable," said Nancy.

Louise nodded.

"We should have reported our discovery in the tunnel room immediately to the security team." Fitz folded his arms on the table.

Nancy blushed. "I'm afraid you're right, but I took a lot of photos of the scene and tried dusting for fingerprints. The shelving is still down there. Security could dust those for prints."

"Hindsight," scoffed Louise. "We were worried it might disappear if we didn't take charge. Anyway, it's done now." Louise looked up as the server stopped at their table for their selections. She ordered the coconut fried shrimp with ambrosia salad and green beans.

Nancy ordered a strip steak with broccoli and Fitz opted for the fried trout, buttered potatoes, and pickled beets.

"Food is still good here," Fitz said, "no matter what else is going on."

"Back to business." Louise looked at Nancy. "Have you made any headway in matching what we found with items residents have reported missing?"

"I could only be partly sure of five items. I photographed them and wrote down the possible names and apartment numbers. We can call on them after dinner."

"Hand me the phone." Louise glanced across the dining room at George. "Let's pretend we're engrossed in the case and make George wish he were over here."

"We need George back," Nancy commented as she handed over her phone.

Louise shook her head as she perused the photos of the jewelry they had found. "I'm still not going to marry him," she said as she returned the phone.

They finished their meals and lingered as the dining room emptied and the residents moved on to their evening pursuits.

"No classes tonight," said Nancy, "or other entertainment. I checked. We should find most people in their apartments."

"Who's first?"

"Edith and Roscoe Barnes, No. 126." Nancy led the way to the Barnes' apartment. Fitz rapped on the door. They could hear the television inside.

Roscoe opened the door. "Hello. Can I help you?" He took a second look. "It's you, Fitz, and," he peered behind Fitz, "Nancy and Louise. Come on in."

"We got the crime squad here," he called to his wife who sat in the living room. They followed him into the room and greeted the wife.

"Take a load off," Roscoe said, pointing to the sofa. "What's up?"

Nancy handed them her phone showing the photo of a brooch set with one large ruby surrounded by pearls. "Is this your brooch?" she asked. "You reported it missing to Harry."

Edith took the photo and studied it. "I believe it is. Where did you find it?"

"Are there any identifying marks on it so you could be sure?" Nancy asked.

"It was made by Cartier. Check for that name on the back," Edith said, "and you can't see all the pearls in this picture, but twenty small ones were circling the ruby.

"Thank you." Nancy took back her phone. "We need to keep it for a few days to help in the investigation. We'll get it to you as soon as we can."

"You think it was involved in the murder?" Edith asked.

"We don't know," answered Fitz, "but please don't mention this to anyone until we're sure."

"We won't" said Edith. She winked at them as she closed the door behind them.

Once back in the hall, Nancy said, "This isn't going to work. Let's go back to my apartment."

"We've got four other pieces of jewelry to check with possible owners," Louise objected as she followed Nancy walking briskly down the hall.

"Edith and Roscoe are probably on the phone now telling people we found her missing brooch," said Nancy. "And it's connected to the murder."

"You're right," added Fitz. "I could see the gleam in their eyes. We need to wait to return anything until we're through investigating."

"I guess you"re right," Louise said. "But we did learn something. The jewelry we showed Edith is probably hers, so we can bet that the other jewelry in the lacquered box also belongs to residents here who reported jewelry missing."

"But the unset gemstones we found hidden in the trunk," added Nancy, "were Glinda's. She probably had them long before she moved to Whisperwood."

"We can make a good guess about one thing," said Fitz. "Whoever stole the trunk didn't know it contained a fortune in gems."

Put On Your Dancing Shoes!

Listen and dance to the big band music of local musicians, the Swing Set Boys, this Saturday night, from 7 to 9 p.m. in the auditorium. This is your time to strut your stuff, whirl your gal, and have a great time with this popular band known throughout the state. If you enjoy the evening, tell Life Enrichment Director Violet Velois and she'll line up more evenings like this.

The Whisperwood Breeze,
Newsletter of Whisperwood
Retirement Village

Chapter 18

At ten the next morning, Nancy, Fitz, and Louise met in Louise's apartment in case Nancy's apartment was bugged. Nancy had called George and left a message, but he hadn't responded. She hoped he would show up.

"We're no further ahead in finding Alex's killer," said Louise, as she added sugar to her tea.

"And we have several concerns," said Nancy. She had set up a flip chart in the living room, and they all stared at its blank surface. "I'll write them down."

"One," she wrote. "Who killed Alex Elmo and Sterling Cooper?

"Two," she said as she wrote. "Who hid stolen items in the tunnel room?

"Three. What should we do about the items we found?

"Four. How can we rectify the damage we caused by removing items from a crime scene? I mean the tunnel room. We should have notified the sheriff immediately.

"Five. Can we dust the stolen items for fingerprints? Look for clues on them?"

"All right." Louise studied the chart. "First things first. Let's brainstorm possible killers."

Nancy flipped to a new sheet. "We can rule out Sterling Cooper, since he was murdered, too, unless two murderers are at work here, which is a stretch."

"What about Simon Smythe?" said Fitz. "He and Alex went around together, he knew Sterling, and he had the run of the grounds."

They stared at the board, and then Louise called out. "Bella and Vicki, the weird sisters."

"Since they moved in so recently, I've put them on the list. They've also been conspicuous in their interest in the case," said Nancy. "Which could mean they want the trunk, too. We just hadn't noticed them until they introduced themselves. I'll look them up in my criminal database."

"Why else would they want to hang around George?" Louise asked. "They want to find out what we know." She clamped her jaw shut.

Nancy added Bella and Vicki to the list. "Don Elmo," Nancy suggested.

"Barbara Elmo," chimed in Louise.

"Wait," said Fitz. "Don and Barbara Elmo were Alex's grandparents. They would not have killed their grandson."

Nancy crossed out Barbara and Don Elmo. "I guess the same would go for Glinda's sons, Cary and Clark who were Alex's second cousins. Anyway, they live miles away in Morgantown and showed no interest in the trunk or even the Elmos. Who else?"

"I don't see Cary as a killer, but Clark is an alcoholic and hard up for cash," said Fitz. "He would be vulnerable to temptation."

"I suppose so," agreed Nancy, "but it's a stretch, and I haven't seen either of them around here. There's someone else here that we should consider. Violet Velois."

"Why her?" asked Fitz. "She's doing a great job for Whisperwood."

"She knew Glinda," said Nancy. Then she added across the top of the chart, "Motive" and "Opportunity."

"Sterling can't be the murderer, although I thought he was a good bet, but why was he killed?" Fitz said.

"Easy," said Louise. "He found out who the killer was or maybe recognized someone here who might have a motive."

"Or he was seen as competing for the gems," suggested Nancy. "Anything else?"

No one spoke up.

"Then who had the opportunity to kill Alex?" Nancy held the pen ready.

"Who didn't?" was Louise's glum reply. "That shed was off the new path to the park. It hasn't been paved yet, so few people use it. The killer chose a time and place that was out of the way and made to order for an unseen murder."

"Doesn't necessarily mean the murderer must have lived here long enough to select a good spot. Anyone who looked around the grounds would see the possibilities for their purpose."

Nancy summed it up. "It could have been anyone, even someone from town."

"Yep," said Fitz.

"I don't think we have enough data here to pinpoint someone," said Fitz. "I think that whoever stashed all that stuff in the tunnel is also our killer. Motive is easy. Money. And it seems to me that all of them had the opportunity since they were all seen on the grounds or in the buildings here. "

"I suppose so," conceded Louise reluctantly, "but maybe the killer was looking for the trunk, ran into Alex, saw him as competition, and killed him."

"Except for Alex, anyone looking for the trunk is probably a contemporary of Glinda's," said Nancy. "That means they are old enough to move into Whisperwood. Since word of Glinda's death has just reached a lot of her friends and acquaintances, they would have moved in recently."

"Like Vicki and Bella," Louise said, crossing her arms. "I don't trust those two. They could be pumping George for information while we sit here."

Nancy flipped the sheet of suspects over for a blank sheet. "We don't know where the stones hidden in Glinda's trunk came from or even if they're genuine. What are we going to do about them?"

She waited as the others stared at the blank flip sheet.

"Glinda was paranoid someone would take her things," Louise said with a dismissive wave. "From what I've heard, she grew up as an orphan and very poor. She would want something for security no matter what happened. *Voila*, the gemstones."

Nancy nodded. "Makes sense. When she retired, she came here to be closer to her sons, but she had to have money to move into Whisperwood. I checked with her son Cary, and he says she didn't have a passport and she hadn't traveled out of the country, so I don't see how smuggling would apply."

"I think the loose gemstones we found are genuine." Fitz had found a magnifying glass and was examining several gems through it. "I think I see tiny inclusions. They don't seem to be round bubbles that might occur in glass. We should get a few of those gems appraised to make sure they're genuine. They could be leftovers from costumes she kept because they were pretty but fake."

"We need to drive into town anyway to pick up a couple of security cameras," said Nancy. "We'll take the gems to a jeweler there."

"Yeah," muttered Louise. "We sure don't want to take them to our in-house jeweler, Simon Smythe."

Nancy smiled. "He does have a vested interest, you might say, but he was very helpful last year when he examined my pearls."

***

Immediately after lunch, Nancy suggested to Fitz that they drive down the mountain to the Interstate that would take them to Charleston, West Virginia's capital and a fairly large town.

"That way we'll avoid the small-town gossip," said Nancy, "should anyone see us buying security cameras and having gemstones appraised. People living anywhere near our community would recognize us as Whisperwood residents by our age and lack of local connections. They'd wonder and they'd gossip."

"A lot of people know you as the Whisperwood

detective," Fitz said, "so I agree. On to Charleston. Keep an eye out for anyone following us."

Nancy nodded. "I am. Too many people at Whisperwood watch what we do out of curiosity. They either want to beat us to name the killer or see us catch him.

Fitz glanced at Nancy. "We do have a reputation, Luv, but I don't think anyone but us and Harry know about the gemstones we found."

They took Fitz's blue Cadillac to Charleston. Nancy kept a look-out for any car that might follow them, but only one stayed behind them down the mountain and then veered off and disappeared. Using her phone, Nancy found a store that sold security cameras. They were a popular item and easily purchased.

"It's a simple set-up," the salesperson explained, "connects to your phone." Then he proceeded to tell them about system requirements and other details that made Nancy's eyes glaze over. She zoned out and let Fitz ask the questions.

"We've got miniature recording devices, too," the salesman said. "He pulled open a drawer under the counter and brought out several examples. "Hide one of these in a table centerpiece and you can record the conversation."

"I'll take one of those," Fitz said. 'By the way, do you have a device that detects bugs?"

"Think someone's listening in on you?" the salesman asked. He walked to a different display case and leaned forward with his elbows on the counter. "To get a good bug detector you'll have to pay thousands of dollars and get hours of specialized training."

Nancy looked at Fitz with an arched eyebrow. "A bug detector?"

"I'd like to see how it works, Luv," he said. "Might be useful."

"I could sell you one of these cheap ones," the salesman said, "but they work on radio frequencies and have a short range. They wouldn't detect much."

Fitz studied the assortment of gadgets in the case and shook his head. "I guess we'll have to hunt for bugs ourselves."

"At least we have a better idea of what they look like," said Nancy.

Fitz shrugged. "I don't know, but we ought to be wary of eavesdroppers."

"You've put your finger on it," Nancy said suddenly. "Someone's finding out what we're doing and dropping hints that I pick up in conversations around the building. The four of us aren't blabbing, so where are they coming from?"

"Easy to hide a bug in a room," said the salesman who was avidly listening in. "They can be quite tiny. We've even got one here that fits in a dog's collar."

"We'll just take the cameras," Fitz said. "Thanks for the information."

Nancy was ready to leave. She was more interested in their next errand. She had located online a prestigious jewelry store in Charleston and made an appointment for the jewelry appraisal.

They walked into a bright showroom with displays of jewelry along with sterling silver and gold bowls and serving utensils. A young woman greeted them and took them to a well-lighted cubicle with a double microscope, scale, and other instruments on a counter. An older man, conservatively dressed in a navy suit with a red tie, welcomed them.

"I'm Tom Taylor," he said. "Good to meet you. I'm intrigued. You say you found these hidden in a trunk you found?"

Nancy nodded. "We need this to be confidential," she explained, hoping she could trust this man. "We found these but we don't know if they are genuine. We also would like to learn about their background if possible. We're not interested in an appraisal or in-depth study. We want to know what we've got here. Could be costume fakes for all we know."

Fitz opened the box he had carried into the store and pulled out the jar of stones. Flashes of color sparkled in the bright light of the room.

Taylor gazed at the jar and then peered at Fitz suspiciously. "You say you found these? In a trunk?"

Fitz nodded.

"You found them legitimately?"

"Yes. We agree that all this is unusual and suspicious, but you can call Harry Doyle, administrator of Whisperwood Retirement Village, for a reference. Here's my ID." Fitz showed him his driver's license.

"I see," he said. Taylor picked up the jar and unscrewed the lid. "Mind if I take a closer look?"

"That's why we're here," Fitz said.

"First, let's find out what we have." He pulled the microscope closer to him, picked up a red stone with tweezers, and placed it in a small box. "I'm checking to see if it fluoresces," he said, "and it certainly does." He studied it under the microscope. "Hmmm. Three small inclusions." He looked at Nancy. "They don't affect the rich, red color. This seems to be a fine ruby." He placed it on the scale. "Weight: 1.5 carats."

"It weighs 1.5 carats? That much? But a diamond at that weight would be larger, wouldn't it?" Nancy asked. Her mother's one-carat diamond had seemed huge on Nancy's finger, so she had it redesigned as a pendant although she rarely wore it.

Taylor used the tweezers to move the brilliant stone back and forth in the light. "That's right," he said thoughtfully, "but a ruby weighs more than a diamond, so a ruby that weighs 1.5 carats will look smaller than a diamond of the same weight. I would say this is a ruby of outstanding quality. Let me look at some of the other gems."

He pulled a box out of a drawer and opened it to pluck out a small square of paper. He folded it into an envelope and dropped the ruby inside. On the outside, he wrote in light pencil, "Ruby, strong color, 1.5 carats. He laid this packet aside and used the tweezers to pick up a sparkling dark blue gemstone. "Sapphire?" he muttered to himself.

All in all, he studied ten of the colored gemstones, which turned out to be an assortment of rubies, sapphires, and emeralds. He used the tweezers to separate the stones into small piles by color.

"Now I'll look at these diamonds," he said. "Some of them are fairly large and may have a laser inscription on them, but let me check them first under the UV light. "Good. They fluoresce a deep blue." He showed the fluorescing diamond to Fitz and Nancy. "It's a natural diamond, not lab-grown or synthetic. Then he examined it under the microscope.

"Laser inscription?" asked Fitz, lifting an eyebrow.

"Do you know where these diamonds came from?" Taylor asked.

Fitz and Nancy shook their heads. "We don't know anything about any of these gemstones," Fitz said, "except they were found in an old trunk. We're trying to learn what we're dealing with before we go to the proper authorities."

"If we can identify the rightful owner," put in Nancy, "we can simply return them."

Taylor nodded thoughtfully. "Well, some larger diamonds have laser inscriptions on the girdle that usually can't be seen with the naked eye, but I'll be able to see them with the microscope. They're put on the stones by diamond firms and labs and each place has its distinct format that may help in tracing stolen or recovered diamonds."

"Interesting," said Fitz. "Such an inscription might be helpful for us."

"I'll look at the larger stones for you, Today, almost all large diamonds have grading reports from gem laboratories that describe a diamond by weight, shape, measurements, cutting style, proportions, color, and clarity. The laser inscription would lead us to all that information and tell us who inscribed it."

"We found no paperwork with these gems," said Nancy.

"All right. I'll examine ten of your larger diamonds and note their characteristics on the paper envelope. You can work from that."

Fitz nodded. "Sounds good. If you find a laser inscription, please set that diamond aside with a note about the inscription, and we'll contact the firm that produced it. That will give us a leg up."

"Just a minute," Taylor said. He examined the diamond. "This has a number on the girdle. I"ll look it up. The Gemological Institute of America has a record anyone can access of gems it has graded and lasered. While you're waiting, you can put each stone into a separate envelope. For the ones I haven't examined, label the package with its color only since I won't have determined whether it's ruby, sapphire, or whatever. We'll assume all the stones are genuine, since the ones I've examined are."

"I was putting them back in the jar," said Fitz.

Taylor shook his head. "Don't do that. The harder ones will scratch the softer ones, damaging them and reducing their value."

He spent a few minutes at an online site. "Unfortunately, this wasn't done by the GIA. I'll have to do more research. Sorry."

"Could we do that?" asked Nancy.

"Better let me handle it."

By the time they left, Fitz carried a box of individually wrapped gemstones and the promise of a complete report on the selected laser-encrypted diamonds in a few days. Nancy paid Taylor for his time and expertise, and they headed home.

"I had no idea how valuable these gemstones were. Glinda had quite a nest egg," said Fitz. "We have to safeguard them until we sort all this out."

"We'll take them back to Harry to return them to

the office safe."

"Good. Harry is young and naive, I'm sorry to say," Fitz glanced at her, "but he's an excellent administrator and trustworthy."

"A pleasant, honest man," agreed Nancy. "I hope Taylor's report will give us the information we need to find out where these gemstones came from."

"We are talking about establishing provenance," Fitz said, "which should tell us who bought them.

"And how Glinda got them."

"And finally, who owns them."

Sign Up Now!
Bus Tour of Charleston, WV
Ed and Mabel King will lead an all-day tour by comfortable bus to West Virginia's capital city, Charleston, founded in 1788. The city is located at the confluence of the Elk and Kanawha rivers. The downtown riverside complex features the gold-domed state capitol, the governor's mansion, and the West Virginia State Museum and Theater. The tour will include lunch and a play, to be announced. Sign up with Ashley at the reception desk. Space is limited.

The Whisperwood Breeze,
Newsletter of the Whisperwood
Retirement Village

Chapter 19

They returned to Whisperwood two hours before their usual dinner time.

"First thing I'm going to do," said Fitz, "is a visual sweep of our apartment now that I know what spy cameras and recorders look like."

"The salesman showed us one the size of a quarter," said Nancy.

"I still ought to be able to see it," Fitz said as he unscrewed their landline phone's transmitter. He showed the dismantled unit to Nancy. "Nothing." He checked the planters, draperies, furniture, ceiling, walls, pictures, and other items but didn't discover any cameras or listening devices.

Nancy took advantage of the time to run a check on Bella and Vicki through Google, Facebook, and a criminal database. She found Bella on Facebook, but nothing on Vicki, yet Vicki seemed smarter and more capable than Bella. Vicki should have some kind of Internet presence. Unless, Nancy mused, Vicki wasn't her real name. Neither appeared in her criminal databases. Bella's Facebook postings were the typical banal drippings along the lines of "I'm fine; how are you?" Vicki was not on Facebook.

Meanwhile, Fitz worked on downloading the security camera app on his cell phone. Nancy ignored the frustrated cursing as he tried to run the app and connect it to the security camera. "Never as easy as they say," he muttered. He picked up the instruction sheet that came with the camera. "It says here that a remote viewing experience on your phone should be simple and enjoyable. Ha!"

He set the camera up, customized the settings for motion detection and alert frequency, and then tested the system on his phone. He was pleasantly surprised when he found himself watching a video of Nancy peering at her computer.

"It works," he called delightedly to Nancy, waving the phone at her. "It actually works."

She looked up. "Great. We can install it tonight."

"And not a moment too soon," said Fitz.

***

At dinner that night, Louise joined them at their regular table fifty-six, but George had again defected "to the dark side," as Louise put it. George walked in with the two women several minutes after the 90s Club had been seated. He never once looked their way.

"We've got the security camera and are ready to set it up," said Nancy, watching as Fitz rummaged through the small flower centerpiece and checked under the table.

"What's he doing?" asked Louise.

"Looking for bugs," Nancy said.

George's defection had knocked Nancy's glee over their successful run to Charleston down a peg.

She could see Louise was trying to hide her feelings behind a phony smile. They went through the usual routine of ordering wine and their meals. Then Fitz told Louise about the cameras.

"Later tonight, we're going down to install them in the basement and the tunnel room."

"I'll go with you to keep watch," said Louise. She glanced across the dining room. "Damn it, I miss George. He would love this."

"I'm worried about him, too," Nancy said, "but he'll get over it when they bore him enough."

"Back to business," Fitz said. "We can't put up the cameras until everyone is out of the basement. We'll have to repeat the drill we went through the other night. We'll meet down there as the classes end and hide. When the basement is cleared, we can work."

"Okay," Louise said." I'll be there before nine."

"Good. In the meantime," Nancy patted Louise's arm, "I'm going to join George and his entourage and find out what's going on."

Louise turned to her with relief. "Would you? I'm so worried about George. I had no idea my refusal would send him off the deep end."

"Wait a minute." Fitz held up a hand. "I should be the one to join George. I can talk to him buddy to buddy, you know? I might also be able to ingratiate myself with the women and find out something more about them."

"Shallow waters there," said Louise, "but tell him we miss him. We need him back on our team."

"Yes, we do," agreed Fitz.

That settled, Nancy told Louise about their visit

to Tom Taylor, the jeweler in Charleston.

"Those gemstones are real," Nancy said, "and fine quality. Tom is sending a report that I hope we can use to track down where Glinda got them and who owns them. Knowing her penchant for thievery and blackmail, I can't believe she got those stones legitimately."

"The jeweler's connections are our best hope," added Fitz. He had kept one eye on George and his group. "They're getting up to leave," Fitz said. "Show time." He left to follow George into the hall.

"Good luck," said Louise and turned to Nancy. "I'm going to my apartment for a quick nap. I'll see you in the basement before nine." To avoid George and Fitz, standing together at the elevator, she strolled past them to the stairs.

Nancy caught up with the sisters ambling down the hall. "Nice evening," she said as they greeted her.

"George has been telling us all about your little 90s Club," warbled Bella. "We'd like to join, but of course, we've both got a long way to go to be that old."

That's meant to be an insult, Nancy thought, amused, but what had George been telling these women? The 90s Club long ago had agreed to keep their activities confidential unless and until necessary. "We like to keep busy," Nancy said. "I've been meaning to find time to get to know you both. How about meeting for lunch tomorrow in the Pub?"

"We'd like that," said Vicki.

"Will this be like a sorority initiation?" put in Bella, hands on hips. "To see if we're good enough?"

"Good enough for what?" asked Nancy, puzzled.

Bella tossed her head. "The 90s Club, of course."

"I wanted a chance to get to know you better." Nancy forced a laugh. "Nothing to do with the 90s Club. That's an informal group, but we have rules and use our skills and experience to fulfill our mission. Any new member would have to have certain skills that would complement those of the others. It's hard, tedious work, often boring, and sometimes danger-ous. We must be able to rely on each other, which is why membership is closed." She hoped that tap dance would put off Bella and Vicki.

"Really?" said Vicki. "I had no idea..."

"But that doesn't mean we can't be friends," Nan-cy said brightly. "How about the Pub at noon."

"All right," said Bella, still pouting. "At noon."

"Fine. See you then." Nancy slowed and let the two women stroll ahead down the hall.

Bella looked back. "I hope Louise can come, too."

"I'll see." Nancy waved and turned around to stride the opposite way to her apartment to wait for Fitz and nine p.m.

He returned an hour later and sank onto the couch.

"How is George?" Nancy asked.

"All right. I caught him up on what we've been doing."

"Was that wise?" Nancy asked. "I met up with the sisters in the hall, and Bella said he's been telling them about us and our activities."

"Really? George told me he's doing undercover work on them because he felt awkward being around Louise right now. He told me not to worry."

"What did he find out?"

"They moved in a month ago," Fitz said, "and have been joining a lot of different groups to keep busy."

"So the 90s Club was one of many."

"Apparently."

"What did they do before coming here?"

"George said they've been cagey about that, although you won't believe this." Fitz paused.

"What?" Nancy asked.

"Bella had been an entertainer before she retired and had met Glinda in Alaska when she worked on a cruise ship one summer."

"Wow. Another link to Glinda," Nancy said. "But will we be getting George back any time soon?"

"He's enjoying being fawned upon and flattered and pampered for a change." Fitz laughed. "The sisters are old school, I guess."

"Or they're up to something." Nancy glanced at the clock. "We should head to the basement. Will George join us?"

Fitz shook his head. "Not tonight. I didn't mention it to him."

"Good," said Nancy. "As long as he is hanging around with the sisters, the less he knows, the better." Fitz picked up the cameras, and they strolled hand in hand to the elevator to head for the basement.

Louise was waiting for them at the elevator. As Nancy and Fitz approached her, she frowned and her gaze went beyond them. Nancy turned, hearing the click click of high heels on the tiled floor behind her.

Nancy's new neighbor Caroline Richards hurried

to catch up with them at the elevator. "I just signed up for an art workshop, so I'm heading to the basement to see what the classrooms are like." She caught up to Nancy, Fitz, and Louise. "Are you taking classes down there, too?"

While Fitz and Nancy fumbled a response, Louise stepped forward. "They were coming down to see the project I'm working on," she said. "But I just told them I've already put it away." She smiled at Nancy. "Next time. We might as well go back to our rooms. I'm tired." She yawned and held up her watch. "Anyway, the classes are over. Everyone's coming back upstairs and heading for their apartments."

"We'll try again tomorrow," said Nancy.

"I guess I'll wait, too," said Caroline. She grinned at Nancy. "Did you have a good time in Charleston?" she asked.

Nancy glanced at Fitz. He shook his head. He hadn't told Caroline they'd gone to Charleston. How had she known? "What makes you think we went to Charleston?" she asked.

Caroline's eyes opened wide. "Saw you in town heading for the Interstate and guessed. I'm always making assumptions. Silly me. So you didn't go to Charleston?"

"Out for a drive," Fitz replied firmly, but Nancy felt hemmed in by inquisitive eyes watching and waiting.

They headed back to their apartment and bade Caroline a good night.

"See you tomorrow," Caroline said.

As soon as Caroline entered her apartment and

closed the door, Nancy opened and shut her own apartment door, and then she and Fitz snuck back to the elevators.

The few stragglers remaining in the basement were soon gone. Nancy and Fitz set to work.

Fitz removed the screw that held the hidden door in place and opened it. A motion light turned on as they descended the stairs and looked for a secure hiding place for the camera.

"We want to capture their faces as they come down the stairs, not their backs," said Fitz. He spotted a niche several feet to the side of the stairs. "Perfect." He then used wire and screws to secure the tiny camera. It was practically invisible.

Nancy nodded with satisfaction. "They probably won't notice it," she said, "but what if they do and destroy it?"

"It turns on when it detects motion and records everything on my phone, which I have here." Fitz pulled out his phone and gave the camera a quick test. "It works," he said, almost as surprised as Nancy. "I got it to work in the apartment, but I always expect frustration and problems when I deal with electronic devices."

"It should be easy. It's like a nanny cam but smaller," said Nancy.

"The man we bought it from showed me exactly what to do," explained Fitz. "I'd already been checking them out online and had watched a video on how to set it up. I was prepared."

"Let's put up the one in the hall," said Nancy. "That might be tricky since there's so much activity during the day and few places to hide it."

Fitz nodded as he set about closing the end wall door. "I'll attach it to the Exit sign at the elevator and train it on the hidden door. Not sure it will do the job but we'll wait and see."

"If anyone spots it, they'll assume the security team installed it," Nancy said. "They won't connect it to us or the secret room."

"No one will have any reason to worry about it except the thief," added Fitz. "He or she might want to dismantle it, but it will be too late."

They were done in five minutes and were waiting at the elevator when it opened and Caroline walked out.

"What are you two doing down here?" she asked.

Nancy glanced at Fitz. "We didn't feel like turning in so early," she stammered. "Decided to come down and view the exhibits." She added with a disappointed tone, "Louise's project isn't on display, though." She waved at the windows where students exhibited their projects.

"I needed a walk, too," said Caroline, "but I didn't expect the basement to be so spooky with the lights turned down. Glad you're here."

They made a show of admiring the crafts before the three agreed it was time for bed.

When they returned to the apartment, Nancy called Louise.

"Did you get the job done?" asked Louise.

"Now we wait for the next step." Nancy spoke in guarded language because of the possible bug listening in. "Thank goodness Fitz got everything done quickly, so we avoided an audience."

"That woman is a nuisance," Louise said.

"By the way, Louise," Nancy said, "I've lined up lunch in the Pub with the two sisters. Want to join us?"

"My, my," said Louise. "How did you get rail-roaded into that? They are definite suspects in my book. Our Georgie has found himself a nest of vipers."

Nancy could hear the venom in Louise's voice.

"Of course, I'll be there." Louise laughed. "Got to check out the competition."

Newcomers Afternoon Tea

Everyone who has moved to Whisperwood since January is invited to the semiannual afternoon tea party in the dining room on Sunday afternoon. Meet and get to know your friends and neighbors at Whisperwood. There will be open seating but each table will include a long-time resident to answer any questions you have about living here. A variety of teas and pastries will be served. Please sign up for this event at the reception counter.

The Whisperwood Breeze,
Newsletter of Whisperwood
Retirement Village

Chapter 20

Nancy was first to arrive at the Pub and ordered her usual iced tea and BLT at the bar. She secured a back table and sat down to wait.

Louise showed up next and also ordered before joining Nancy. "Maybe they won't show," Louise grumbled.

They waited. Their BLTs and iced teas arrived, and as they began eating, Vicki and Bella walked in, fifteen minutes late. They waved as they spotted Nancy and Louise and came directly to the table.

"They're putting us in our place," Louise whispered to Nancy. "We should finish and leave."

But Nancy was curious about the two women. "Order at the bar," she told them. "You'll get your food faster."

"Oh, we never do that," Bella said. "We demand to be served." She and her sister took seats at the table.

"Where are you from?" put in Louise, rolling her eyes as she glanced at Nancy.

"Virginia. Arlington," said Vicki. "I worked for the government. Bella was a hair stylist when she wasn't getting gigs as a singer."

"I was a very popular singer, you know, in Washington, New York, Chicago, and I even worked a few cruise ships," Bella said.

"How did you find this place?" Nancy asked.

Vicki set down her glass. "We were born in West Virginia, but the eastern panhandle part, which is more like a Washington suburb now." She laughed.

Bella stepped in. "We picked up a promotional brochure on Whisperwood, and it made this place seem delightful, so when we retired, we pooled our money and moved here."

"We've met very interesting people so far," Vicki said. With a sly glance at Nancy, she added, "Some are friendlier than others."

"George is such a nice man." Bella tittered. "We're glad he's been joining us for dinner. We're planning some outings around the countryside."

"Good for you," muttered Louise, sourly.

Bella looked around. "Where is the server?" she pouted.

"I told you," Louise said irritably. "They're slow here. Faster if you order your food at the bar. They'll bring it to the table."

Bella frowned. "I'm used to better treatment."

"Never mind." Vicki got up. "I'll order for us."

Nancy watched her stalk to the bar. Vicki and Bella had not been at Whisperwood long enough to find out about the tunnel room. The long-time residents knew Whisperwood rested on an old mining site, but they were told the tunnels had been blocked off and not accessible. That's what Vicki and Bella would have heard if the subject came up. Even Nancy and

Fitz had believed it until they found the secret tunnel room.

Bella interrupted her thoughts. "Do you have suggestions for interesting places to visit around here?" she asked.

"Try the new path that goes past the gardens at Whisperwood," Nancy said. "It connects to the public park and is a lovely walk." Bella and Vicki had shown up suspiciously close to the time when Sterling and Alex appeared. Had they all come here for the same reason? To find Glinda's gemstones? How connected were the four of them? How did Simon Smythe fit in? She didn't believe Barbara and Don knew anything about the gems. They had shown no interest and had let the trunk go when they had it.

What had triggered the sudden arrival of these strangers, each with some connection to Glinda?

Vicki returned to the table with two Cokes. "Orders are in," she said.

"Did you ever meet Glinda or her sister Barbara?" asked Nancy. "Or her nephew Alex, the man who was murdered here?"

Bella glanced at Vicki. "We were delighted to meet Barbara, and I met her sister when we both toured as performers with a cruise line in Alaska. But we have heard their hard luck story. They had a tough life growing up, those two."

"Barbara told us about Glinda one day when we met for tea. She's still finding it difficult to get over Glinda's being murdered," Vicki said. "We're sisters, too. We understand."

"What about Alex and Sterling," Louise said.

"Did you ever meet them before?"

Vicki shrugged. "Not that I recall. This place seems so secure and peaceful and yet both those poor men were murdered on the grounds or nearby. How could that happen with all the security around?"

Bella fluttered her hands. "Let's not talk about that terrible murder. We're new here and had nothing to do with those disasters."

Vicki ignored her and turned piercing eyes on Nancy. "George says you are a retired detective."

Nancy nodded. "That's true, but I retired a long time ago. I'm not up to date, what with DNA testing and other current techniques."

"But he says he's part of the 90s Club," Vicki pursued, "along with you and your fiancé and Louise here, and you saved Whisperwood by catching a couple of murderers."

Louise laughed. "Everybody knows Nancy's cat Malone is the one who caught the criminals."

"We simply try to help local law enforcement," added Nancy, "if we can." Had these women pushed George like this? She hoped he hadn't caved and revealed details of their current investigation to his new friends.

"We don't understand why you don't want our help," said Vicki. "What are you doing to find Alex's murderer?" Her intent expression told Nancy that Vicki had come to the real agenda of this lunch meeting.

"Sorry. Can't talk about it." Louise rapped the table.

Nancy smiled apologetically. "We simply keep our eyes and ears open. We aren't real detectives."

She finished her sandwich. "Sorry, but I have to go."

"Me, too," Louise said.

As they walked out of the Pub, Louise muttered, "We better talk to George. Those women will play on his ego to weasel everything we're doing out of him."

"And to keep him away from us," Nancy added.

Happy Hour at the Pub
4 to 5 p.m.
Monday through Friday
Join your friends and enjoy a
relaxing interlude before dinner.
2 for 1 drinks!

Ad in *The Whisperwood Breeze,*
Newsletter of Whisperwood
Retirement Village.

Chapter 21

Louise waved goodbye to Nancy and pressed the elevator button. "Got to put on my beekeeping outfit and check on my employees," she joked.

Nancy walked on to her apartment where she found Fitz watching Malone and Cleo bat a crumpled piece of paper around the living room.

"Caroline should be back soon to pick up Cleo," Fitz said. "How did your lunch date go?"

"There's something off about those two sisters," Nancy said. "They tried to pump us, and I'll bet they're doing that with George. We need to caution him."

"With George's battered ego, he's vulnerable to that kind of thing." Fitz caught the paper and threw it into the kitchen. The cats scampered after it.

Nancy watched their antics with a smile. "I always thought Malone was a loner."

"He likes Cleo."

Nancy heard a knock on the door.

"There she is now." Nancy welcomed Caroline in. "The cats are having a good time," she said.

Cleo ran into the living room and halted as she saw Caroline. The words "Uh oh" crossed her face as clearly as if she'd spoken. Caroline scooped her up quickly before she could disappear because that was obviously Cleo's intent.

"Time to come home," Caroline crooned as she cuddled her little kitty.

Once she had gone, Fitz and Nancy left to visit George. They found him in his apartment pecking away at the computer. His surprise was evident as he opened the door. "To what do I owe this rare visit?" he asked.

"We miss you, George," said Nancy as she walked in.

"I needed a break." He ran a hand over his bald head. "So I decided not to join you for dinner."

"Is this still about Louise?" Fitz asked.

Nancy watched George for a reaction. Louise's refusal of his proposal had to hurt, but George only chuckled.

"Fiddle-faddle. I knew she'd refuse me, but it was worth the effort," George said, "just to see the look on her face."

"What?" Nancy exclaimed.

"I wanted to shake things up a little." He waved at his computer. "And anyway, I've been working on my novel."

"Louise is upset and worried about you," said Nancy, taking a seat in the living room. Fitz and George followed her lead.

"Why? I can take care of myself." George sat back with folded arms. "Those two women were pestering me to sit with them, so I did. Change of pace. That's all."

"We're worried about their motives," Fitz said.

George nodded. "And you think with my so-called bruised ego, I'd be putty in their hands?"

"Yes. Louise and I had lunch with them today," said Nancy, "and they tried to pump us about the murders."

"I'm sure they did. I'm onto them." George got up to pace the room. "I don't tell them anything about our work. I bore them with computer lessons, which they try hard to appear interested in."

Nancy saw the twinkle in his eye and felt vastly relieved. He was still their George.

"I'm your undercover operative." George grinned and flexed his muscles. "So tell me what's been happening."

Fitz told George about the cameras they had installed in the tunnel room and the basement.

"And we checked the gemstones with a jeweler in Charleston," added Nancy. "They seem to be genuine," added Nancy. "Worth a fortune."

"Quite a haul." George nodded. "Alex and Sterling knew all about what was in that trunk, but they were too new here to know about the hidden door to the tunnel."

"Why didn't the person who hid the trunk know about the gems, too?" asked Nancy.

"Why would he?" said Fitz. "He probably thought he might get a few bucks selling it as an antique."

"Well, anyway," George rubbed his hands together. "Alex and Sterling are dead, and we've got the trunk and the rocks. So now what kind of trap can we set to catch the killer?"

Feeling Stressed? Need a Break?
Join Lois Champion's Yoga and Meditation Class held each week on Monday and Friday from ten a.m. until noon. Spend an hour working with Lois on exercises to stretch and limber your body, then an hour in guided meditations, contemplation, and poetry to exercise and expand your mind.

The fee for the eight-week session is $75 or you can drop in for $10 a session. Register with Ashley at the reception desk.

The Whisperwood Breeze,
Newsletter of Whisperwood
Retirement Village

Chapter 22

George was back at their regular table in the dining room that evening. Nancy was amused to see Louise modify her usual brashness and sarcasm in an effort to please George. He wore a lemon-colored dress shirt with a blue polka-dot bowtie. It made Nancy smile. George was his old self again.

The pall that had settled on their table in George's absence lifted. Louise even smiled at George. Everything was back to normal.

Fitz again checked the centerpiece and under the table for bugs. "All clear," he said, "but everyone knows we sit at this table most nights. It's worth checking."

They gave their wine orders to the dining room manager and perused the menu. The server filled their water glasses and hovered. They were all eager to discuss the case, so they made short work of submitting their orders. When the wine came, Louise offered a toast to the four of them. Their glasses clicked and they drank.

"What's next?" asked George, peering at them as

he set down his glass.

"I'm working on checking the residents' descriptions of their lost items," said Nancy, "with the lists of the pieces we discovered in the tunnel."

Louise sipped her wine and looked up. "What about Glinda's pebbles, the ones in the jar?"

"Hey, what are we doing about them?" George asked.

"We're waiting for the jeweler's appraisal, Nancy explained to George. "Some of the larger diamonds have laser tags indicating who produced them."

"Once we know that," added Fitz, "we can contact the laser lab and find out to whom they sold the diamonds."

"We want to know how Glinda got them," said Nancy. "Were they gifts? Did she buy them? Were they stolen? Who gets them now?

George folded his arms on the table. "You know," he said, "that history is beside the point. The trunk was part of Glinda's estate. That means whatever was in the trunk was part of the estate, too. Didn't her sons inherit her estate?"

"I think so," Nancy said, not liking where George was going.

"Check that out to be sure, then hand the gemstones over to the heir. No problem." George clapped his hands. "Case closed."

"You're right, George," Nancy conceded, "but I'm curious. Aren't you? Alex, Sterling, and someone else, the killer, were after those stones. How did they learn about them? Glinda was murdered a year ago. What happened that now, a year later, they came to

Whisperwood looking for them?"

George started to respond, but Nancy held up her hand. "And why didn't Barbara, Don, Cary, and Clark know about them? They were her closest kin."

Again, George tried to speak, but Louise interrupted. "Don't forget we're after the thief as well as the murderer of Alex Elmo and Sterling Cooper. Those rocks played a part. We need to keep them until the thief and the killer are caught."

George held up his hands in surrender. "All right," he said. "Where did you put them?"

"In Harry's safe," Fitz said. "We counted each gem before we left Harry's office, and in the jewelry store, we listed each gem and put it into a little envelope."

"You know the thief may have nothing to do with the murders," drawled Louise.

"That's possible, but we still have to pursue that avenue." Nancy sat back as the server placed their orders around the table.

"Louise and I found Alex dead behind the garden at one of the storage sheds," she said. "That was at nine-thirty a.m."

"Harry confided to me," Fitz said, "that the bullet recovered was a nine mm."

"A lot of guns use nine mm bullets," commented Nancy. "As we all know, when we moved in here, we were notified of Whisperwood's no firearms policy. That doesn't mean someone might have one anyway, so we can't rule out a resident."

"The only non-resident on our suspect list was Sterling Cooper," Louise said.

"He was staying in a motel in town," said Fitz, "but I saw him roaming the halls here and eating lunch with Simon, Barbara, and Don."

Nancy nodded. "I've seen them together, too. Anyway, he's one of the victims, so he can't be the murderer."

"I wonder how the sheriff's investigators are doing," Louise said.

George shook his head. "You know they won't tell us anything."

"Not us," Nancy said, "but maybe Ashley."

The other three stared at Nancy, shocked.

"Ashley?"

"The receptionist?"

"No way."

"Why not?" Nancy said. "She's an adult, lives in town, and knows where the sheriff's men hang out. I'll bet she'd love to help us out, and there'd be no danger for her."

Light gradually dawned on the other faces.

"It might work," said George.

"I'll talk to her tomorrow," said Nancy.

Special Notice to the Residents
Contribute Now to
Whisperwood's Scholarship Fund

This June, four Whisperwood dining room servers will graduate from high school. Two are planning on college. Whisperwood has a tradition of providing each graduating senior with a scholarship or monetary gift that can be used for college, job training, starting a business, or any other educational or job opportunity.

These scholarships are funded by your generous support. Our students serve you faithfully every day in our dining room. No employee at Whisperwood receives tips.

Please help give our students a well-deserved graduation gift. Submit your contribution to Gene Reynolds, finance director, or drop it off at the reception desk.

Harry Doyle, Administrator

Chapter 23

Nancy set up her information table in the lobby the next morning. The questions from residents about scams and frauds had dwindled, thanks to the lectures by West Virginia's consumer agencies and Nancy's help. She still maintained the table, and both Harry and Ashley were glad to have someone else run interference with residents' repetitive questions.

This time, Nancy bought a small box of donuts and asked Ashley to join her outside for a few minutes. "We can share the donuts."

"Sure," said Ashley. "Nothing's happening here. What's up?" She grabbed a cup of coffee and followed Nancy out the front door.

Nancy led Ashley to the garden bench where they could talk privately. "You live in town," Nancy began, passing the donut box to Ashley. "We, that is, the 90s Club, are wondering if you know any of the sheriff's officers."

"Aha!" said Ashley. "You want me to find out what's going on with the murder investigation."

"You've got it," said Nancy. No doubt about it, Ashley was quick.

"As it so happens," Ashley said with a smile, "my brother Jimmy works for the county, and he went to high school with Buddy Youngblood, who is a deputy in the sheriff's office. I got connections."

"Wonderful. Exactly what we hoped." Nancy raised her hand for a high five.

"It'll cost you," said Ashley, grinning.

"What do you want?" Nancy glanced appraisingly at Ashley.

Ashley laughed. "I want to be an honorary member of the 90s Club. I see a lot in the lobby. I can help you guys."

"Let's see how this assignment goes, but you're right. You're in a position to hear casual conversations and meet people who could be useful to us in our investigations. Right now, we want to find out what the sheriff's office is doing since they won't tell us anything. Do they have any suspects or clues? Have they found the gun? Uncovered any motives? We're ready to help. We know the players, the possible suspects and the history. The sheriff and his deputies could use our help."

"I get it. I've seen you guys in action. I can find out anything you want to know about our fair city, too. You're stuck here and don't know many people in town." Ashley finished the donut and wiped her hands on a napkin. "If I help you out with this, then you'll make me a member?"

"Help us with this case, and I'll talk to the other members about future assignments," Nancy said, smiling at Ashley's enthusiasm, "but we could use your help and I don't see why not."

"I'll talk to Jimmy tonight and report tomorrow." Ashley stood. "Now I've got to get back to work."

Nancy followed Ashley into the lobby, retrieved her laptop and sign, and walked back to her apartment. Fitz had gone out early on a bird-watching hike and hadn't returned. Nancy opened her laptop and found Tom Taylor's report on the gemstones in her email.

It included the contact information for the diamond laboratory that had put laser tags on Glinda's larger diamonds. Taylor had asked the labs for further information on the tagged diamonds, but the lab supplied only certificates of the quality or grade of each diamond submitted. Those diamonds were like a car with a license tag, Nancy thought, but who owned the diamonds? Where had Glinda gotten them? What about the other stones? Were they connected to the diamonds or from somewhere else? How could they find out? Nancy decided another visit to Charleston was necessary.

When Fitz returned from the hike, she discussed this with him.

"Okay," he said. "I'll call Taylor and suggest we meet for lunch to discuss what we've learned.

The next day, Fitz and Nancy made another trip to Charleston and easily found the Black Diamond Pub, suggested by Taylor. It was an upscale downtown restaurant where napkins were black or white depending on the color of the patron's trousers or skirt.

Taylor was already seated when they arrived and rose as he and Fitz shook hands. Both men ordered local beers while Nancy had an iced tea. "I'm driving back," she said but heartily approved of the beer for the men. She wanted a relaxed and cordial lunch with a positive atmosphere.

They ordered and then Taylor folded his arms on the table and looked at them. "What's up?" he asked.

"Thank you very much for sending us the reports on the diamonds," said Nancy, "but they weren't very helpful."

"I didn't think they would be." Taylor sipped the beer and sat back. "They did show the diamonds were top quality, but no kind of provenance."

"We need to know who owns them," Nancy said.

Fitz leaned forward and told him about Glinda and the recent interest in her antique trunk.

"You're saying she was murdered and then her trunk disappeared?" Taylor asked. "And now a year later people have appeared at Whisperwood looking for it? Why?"

"Exactly," said Fitz. "We think we know why." He paused to sip his beer. "We found the trunk and those gemstones we brought to you were hidden in the trunk's screw holes."

"The screw holes? How did that work?"

"They were drilled too deep," Nancy jumped in, "and filled in with the stones along with protective batting. There was also a false bottom to the trunk."

"I see. And what does this have to do with me?" asked Taylor as their sandwiches arrived.

Nancy glanced at Fitz. "We don't know where those gemstones came from. We don't even know if Glinda owned them or was being used to smuggle them for some reason. She could have stolen them."

Fitz stepped in. "The lab report on the lasered diamonds didn't provide any kind of provenance."

"As I told you," Taylor said, "I didn't know to ask about ownership. The lab can probably give us the name of the individual or company who requested the inscription, then we'd have to contact them."

"We could call them," Fitz said.

"Better let me call," Taylor said. "It's confidential information. I gather the sheriff's officer doesn't know about these stones?"

"Not yet." Fitz bit into his sandwich. "We do need to find out who owns the stones and we'll have to get that from you."

"No problem since you're the ones who brought the stones to me in the first place."

"Of course, we will turn the trunk and gemstones over to the sheriff's office," Nancy added. "We have a complete list of the stones we found, a description of the trunk, and the lab's report in case a discrepancy appears in the sheriff's records."

"We don't know how tight a ship they run there," Fitz said. "And the trunk was found with other jewelry and articles that residents at Whisperwood have reported missing. We're helping Whisperwood's administrator sort that out."

Was Taylor buying this story? Nancy couldn't tell. Feeling desperate to engage him on their side, she elaborated. "Four of us—we call ourselves the 90s Club—have solved other crimes at Whisperwood. We're on the scene and know the residents. We could provide valuable help to the sheriff and his investigators, but they aren't interested despite the help we've given them in the past. We have to go it alone."

"Glinda's nephew was murdered at Whisperwood a week ago." Fitz finished his sandwich and pushed the plate aside. "He was one of the men inquiring about Glinda's trunk. At that time, no one knew where it was. We think that trunk and its hidden gemstones are the reason for his murder."

Taylor finished his sandwich, too, pushed the plate aside, and folded his arms on the table. "That's quite a story."

"There's more," said Nancy, nodding at Fitz.

"The metal straps that decorate the trunk are mostly brass," Fitz said, "but some of the brass is painted over with black lacquer. But underneath that lacquer on one fitting the metal is actually gold. We think it's like 14-karat or 18-karat gold."

"I'm interested," said Taylor. "As it happens, my aunt lives at Whisperwood. She told me all about you and your, ah, exploits. I'll help you, but you must agree to turn over the trunk, the gemstones, and the information you've gathered to the police within a week of my sharing it with you."

Nancy nodded. "That's fair. We plan to do that anyway."

"And you have to tell me what happens."

Fitz grinned. "Sure. We'll come back and give you the full story."

Taylor rose. "You got a deal. Say hello to my aunt, Mildred Koontz, will you? She'll be thrilled."

Lost Anything Lately?
Whisperwood's box of found objects
is full of your missing umbrellas, hats,

watches, shoes, gloves, jewelry, and other items. On July 1, all items in the "Found Box" will be discarded or taken to the thrift shop. If you've lost something at Whisperwood, fill out the "Lost and Found" form at the reception desk with a description and your name and phone number. If we see any item resembling the one you lost, we will call you to identify it and pick it up. Remember: Deadline for claiming a found item is July 1.

The Whisperwood Breeze,
Newsletter of Whisperwood
Retirement Village.

Chapter 24

The next morning Nancy went outside for an early walk on the path to the county park. The weather was cool and dry, and she was pleased to see another walker ahead of her. It turned out to be Simon Smythe.

"Enjoying the weather?" she asked pleasantly.

"It's nice enough," Simon said with a casual glance toward the gate. Nancy was glad to see a guard on duty there.

Simon continued walking. "The sheriff's investigator is trying to pin Alex's murder on me, but I barely knew the guy."

"Why does he think that?" Nancy asked.

He shrugged. "I guess we were seen together here and in town by some nosey parkers."

Probably true. This was a small town. Everyone knew everyone else. Gossip was rampant. But Whisperwood and its residents generally bought locally and had a good reputation with the local citizens, despite the big city problems like murder that had occurred at Whisperwood.

"You knew him in Alaska, didn't you?"

"In my early days, I went to Alaska to prospect,

but that was a nightmare. I'd always had a flare for drama and took up with a local theater group. Glinda and Sterling happened to be part of the theater network in Anchorage. We were in the same business. Couldn't help meeting them through the theater group and in the bars after performances. That doesn't mean I killed them. Alex was too young and no part of that scene. Met him here."

"Why do you think Alex and Sterling were killed?"

"Alex was a felon. Who knows what kind of trouble he was in? I had nothing to do with him." Simon mimed washing his hands. "I don't have any idea why Sterling was killed."

"He was looking for Glinda's trunk, too. Quite a coincidence, isn't it?" said Nancy, fishing.

"Both of them told me they found out about Glinda's death at the same time—months after the fact." Simon rubbed the stubble on his chin. "News sometimes has trouble catching up to people in Alaska. I'm sorry for Barbara and Don's loss," he flashed an ugly grin at Nancy, "but their grandson was no good."

He thrust out his chin. "Now if you don't mind..." He nodded at Nancy and walked forward, but she stepped in front and blocked him.

"You might consider," she said, "that like Alex and Sterling, you knew Glinda in Alaska and you knew about her trunk. That makes you a suspect. It also makes you a candidate for murder."

"Thank you for the warning," said Simon, "but if I were the murderer, I'd go after you next."

Nancy watched him stride into the building. She continued on her walk. This time, she stopped to chat with the gate guard, who was eating a donut. He held a coffee cup in the other hand.

After the initial pleasantries, Nancy asked him, "Are there many nighttime visitors?"

"No, ma'am," he said. "People, especially visitors, don't like to climb that mountain in the dark. Or go down it, neither."

"Do you mind if I take a look at your check-in log?" asked Nancy.

He sipped the coffee. "Most of the time, ma'am, we don't let just anybody look at the book. Privacy issue, you know. The police? Yeah, that's different. But seeing as how it's you, I'll make an exception." He handed it over.

The log was kept in an ordinary spiral-bound notebook. Lines divided each page into three columns: Date and time; Name; Person Visiting. This log began with an entry two weeks earlier. Nancy glanced through the names. Alex was checked in at two p.m. the day before he was killed and then again early the next morning. Both times, he indicated that he was visiting his grandparents, Barbara and Don Elmo.

Then she noticed a peculiar entry, made a week before Alex died. Someone named Piers Campbell said he was going to visit Bella and Vicki. Piers Campbell worked for the sheriff's office. She continued glancing through the pages but found nothing else of interest. She gave the notebook back to the guard with her thanks.

At nine a.m. Nancy returned to the lobby. Ashley was filling a cup at the coffee bar. She smiled and winked at Nancy as she walked to the reception counter.

"Operative Ashley reporting for duty," she said.

Nancy smiled. "Right on time, too. Did you find out anything?"

She shook her head. "No witnesses. No DNA evidence. No fingerprints. They found a bullet casing about ten feet from the body and recovered a 9 mm bullet lodged in the chest. They asked Harry to distribute a notice asking for anyone with information to come forward." Ashley sipped her coffee. "Check your inbox."

Nancy nodded, biting her lip. "Any suspects?"

"That Sterling Cooper guy was number one suspect until he was killed. Now they're taking close looks at everyone connected to the Elmos." She raised an eyebrow. "Even you."

Nancy laughed. "I'm sure I am a suspicious character. By the way, I met Simon Smythe on the path this morning."

"He has been hanging around the lobby lately." Ashley took a minute to answer a phone call and then continued her report. "The investigator looked into Alex and Sterling's backgrounds and found both had a string of arrests behind them. Those sisters, Bella and Vicki?"

"What about them?" asked Nancy.

"There's something funny going on there," Ashley said. "I notice things here in the lobby, and they hang around a lot, talking to people, asking questions. Too much, if you ask me."

Nancy nodded. *What were those two up to?* "Thanks, Ashley, for your help. Keep your ears open. You're in a good place to find out what's going on and we need to know."

"You betcha," she said.

"By the way, someone named Piers Campbell from the sheriff's office visited Vicki and Bella a few days ago. Can you find out why?"

"Campbell works with Lt. Harmason on investigations like this," Ashley said.

"Thanks," said Nancy. Did the two sisters know something they were sharing only with the sheriff's office? Or was Campbell taking a closer look at them as suspects?

Notice to the Residents
Whisperwood's Got Talent!

Do you sing or play a musical instrument? Are you knowledgeable about a subject of interest to Whisperwood residents? Fill out the Talent Showcase form attached and return it to the reception desk. Life Enrichment Director Violet Velois is planning shows and lectures featuring our residents. This is your time to shine!

The Whisperwood Breeze,
Newsletter of Whisperwood
Retirement Village

Chapter 25

Fitz was working on a project in the apartment while keeping an eye on Malone and Cleo, who were enjoying another play date. Nancy left them to walk to the lobby and relax with a cup of coffee in one of the comfortable armchairs.

She had suggested that Caroline join her at the coffee bar, but Caroline had again gone off to town. This time, she was going to a hairdresser even though Whisperwood had a beauty salon.

"Takes too long here," Caroline said as she left.

It wasn't Nancy's day to staff the information table, but she had nothing else pressing to do. Sometimes she learned a little more about the social dynamics at Whisperwood sitting there and watching the residents come and go.

Eventually, she heard Bella coming down the hall babbling to someone and then saw her stroll into the lobby, hanging onto Simon Smythe's arm. When she saw Nancy, she detached and distanced herself from Simon.

Nancy hid her surprise. How well were Bella and

Simon acquainted?

Bella dropped into the chair beside Nancy. Simon greeted Nancy coldly but took the other chair. To Nancy's amusement, he focused his attention solely on Bella, who had apparently become Whisperwood's new *femme fatale*.

"Has the 90s Club figured out who the killer is yet?" Bella asked with a simpering smile.

"I'm afraid not. The sheriff is the investigator." Nancy sipped her coffee. "He hasn't asked for our help."

"That's not what George says," Bella continued. "He told us you found the trunk everyone's looking for."

"What?" Nancy sputtered, shocked at the statement while also noticing that Simon's attention was suddenly riveted toward her. "That's ridiculous."

Bella shrugged. "That's what George said. He's part of your 90s Club, isn't he? Why would he lie?"

Nancy recovered herself, Knowing she had to navigate this conversation carefully. She assumed a look of concern and reached out to pat Bella's hand in a patronizing way. "Bella, I think you misunderstood something George might have said. It's easy to do since he speaks so softly." She glanced at Simon who was listening intently. "Have you had your hearing checked?"

"Of course not," she replied irritably. "My hearing is perfectly good."

"You misunderstood George, then. I hope you won't repeat such absurd stories. Certainly, if we'd discovered the murderer or the trunk, we would have notified the sheriff."

Nancy appealed to Simon. "You've seen how rumors fly around this place. Bella could only do herself and all of us harm by repeating falsehoods. The killer could even target her next."

Simon stroked his chin. "That's true. Nothing is served by lies, Bella. Keep this nonsense to yourself. If you persist in spreading such stories and time proves them to be lies, you will make yourself an outcast."

Bella pouted. "You two are ganging up against me. I know what I heard, and I don't care what you think." She stood. "I'm going outside for a walk." She left in a huff.

"You don't believe her, do you?" asked Nancy. "Even if what she says were true, George would never discuss it with anyone but the 90s Club."

Simon also rose. "I'm sure you're right," he said.

As soon as Simon disappeared down the hall, Nancy raced to her apartment and called George. George was slow answering and then muttered an irritated "Hello."

"Bella just told me you said we'd found the trunk." Nancy kept her voice bland.

"You interrupted me in the middle of writing my novel for that?" George said. "I don't tell them nothing. I hope you didn't fall for her lies."

"I was in the lobby and she and Simon Smythe sat down next to me. She said you told her that we knew the identity of the murderer and where the trunk is."

"What?" George sputtered. "I did no such thing. I was my usual charming self and talked only about the novel I'm writing and books in general. Nothing, nil, nada about the 90s Club and what we're doing."

"Simon was extremely interested in her comments. Too interested. And she left in a huff, insisting that what she said was true. She's going to spread that story around."

George was silent so long Nancy thought he'd hung up. Finally, he said, "You know what this means, don't you?"

"We're all in danger," Nancy answered. "We need to meet quickly and figure out how to stop her or counter her lies."

"And how to protect ourselves."

***

When Nancy talked to Fitz about a meeting, he didn't immediately agree. "Let me think about it," he said. He held a finger to his lips, scribbled something on a piece of paper, and handed it to Nancy.

She read the message, looked at Fitz, and saw the serious expression on his face. She wrote under his note: "Thank you. I forgot our apartment might be bugged."

He nodded.

She added another message. "Let's meet in Louise's apartment."

He nodded again.

This time Nancy texted Louise and George, and the 90s Club met in Louise's apartment at four p.m., just before dinner. Nancy had relayed to all of them Fitz's suspicions, Bella's comments, and George's denials. "We need to stop or refute her lies," Nancy said. "If the killer hears that we're onto him, or her, he'll target us. The ones who want the trunk or are curious about it will watch us everywhere we go."

"Have the cameras picked up anyone at the end wall in the basement?" asked Louise. "Seems like whoever hid the trunk in the secret room might want to check on it."

"Or else stay away from it entirely," suggested Fitz. "But no, nothing on the cameras yet."

Louise glanced at George. "Did it occur to you that Bella is a troublemaker, making up lies to fish for guilty reactions?"

"If that's what she's doing," Nancy said, "she's playing a dangerous game."

George nodded. "That's what she's doing all right. Fits right in with her character."

Fitz sat back and folded his arms. "The best thing we can do is laugh at her and generally maintain an air of disbelief in anything she says."

"Destroy her credibility, in other words," added Louise.

"Do the same to rumors from other people," said Nancy. "We all know how fast rumors fly in this place."

Nancy studied George. She believed his denials. "George," she said, "you should go back to their table for dinner. Stay close to them and do what you can to stop her."

George sat up and blinked. "You want me to be a...a...mole?"

"You sat with them before," muttered Louise. "You can do it again."

George frowned at her. "Okay, but just this one more time. Vicki's okay, but Bella..." He shuddered

Fitz glanced at his watch. "And now's the time, but there's one other thing..."

"What?" asked Nancy.

"I think this means we can remove Bella and Vicki from our suspect list. They wouldn't be churning the waters and calling attention to themselves if they were guilty."

Nancy nodded and rose along with the others to step toward the door. "You're probably right," she said. "Or they're playing a deeper game in the hunt."

Loose Lips Sink Ships

Recent events at Whisperwood have given rise to harmful and false rumors that breed suspicion and ill feelings among all of us here at Whisperwood. We encourage all residents to maintain a skeptical attitude toward these rumors and to stop their spread. Whisperwood is a kind and friendly place. Let's keep it that way.

The Whisperwood Breeze,
Newsletter of Whisperwood
Retirement Village

Chapter 26

As Nancy fed Malone a mid-morning snack the next day, she heard a knock on the door. Fitz was at the gym. She tossed the treat into a far corner to beat Malone to the door. Vicki Townsend stood in the hall. "I need to talk to you," she said.

"Come in." Nancy stepped aside to let Vicki in, closing the door quickly before Malone could reach it and run out.

"Bella left this morning for a walk and hasn't returned," Vicki said.

Nancy glanced out the window at the sunshine on the flowers. "She's probably enjoying this beautiful weather."

"She had a dental appointment in town at ten-thirty this morning, and it's almost eleven. I called them and they haven't seen her. She was going down to the basement first to look at the crafts displays, but between you and me, I think something funny is going on down there. Then she likes to walk the path into the new park behind the building. I'm afraid she might be hurt." Vicki wrung her hands. "Or worse considering what's been going on here." She shivered.

Vicki glanced at her watch. "She left early to see the basement before classes started. She must have made it to the path by now."

Nancy felt chilled with foreboding. "I'm ready for a walk. Let's go out and find her." Nancy picked up a sun hat and led Vicki into the hall and out the side exit door. The path led past the gardens and Nancy waved to Louise, busy checking her hive. They turned onto the wooded path into the county park. Nancy had expected to see more residents out on this beautiful morning, but the solitude felt peaceful and soothing.

Until Nancy heard a faint moan.

The sound emanated from behind the high-growing bushes beside the path. She peered through the leaves and glimpsed an unnatural and large patch of pink on the ground.

Oh, no, she thought, as an increasing sense of foreboding made her hands tremble. She pushed through the brush and stepped into a clearing to look down on the still body of Bella Shore. Flies buzzed around the blood oozing from the wound on her head.

Vicki followed Nancy into the clearing and immediately knelt beside her sister. She waved the flies away and cradled Bella's head in her arms. "She's alive," said Vicki. "Call 911."

"I forgot my phone," Nancy cried. "I'll be right back." She ran out of the park and onto Whisperwood's land straight to Louise.

Nancy panted, out of breath. "Louise, call 911 for an ambulance and the sheriff. We've just found Bella, and she's been hurt."

"Hurt?" Louise said, staring at Nancy.

"Call 911 and get help, Louise," Nancy repeated. "I'm going back to Bella and Vicki. We're down the path a little ways."

Louise quickly set the hive smoker aside, replaced the cover on the bee hive, and pulled out her phone. "I'm on it," she said.

Nancy returned to Vicki and waited with her for the ambulance and sheriff. Vicki was white-faced and seemed to have shriveled in the minute Nancy had been gone. Someone had hit Bella with a heavy object. Vicki had torn off a leafy branch to wave away the flies, but her sharp eyes darted everywhere.

The emergency vehicles took twenty minutes to arrive from town and then drove across Whisperwood's manicured landscaping and onto the path to stop next to Bella who moaned in Vicki's arms. Vicki stepped back to let the paramedics in, and the three women hung around on the outskirts of the small group of residents who had ambled by and then stayed behind the sheriff's vehicles and ambulance to watch. Nancy listened to the murmured speculation around them, but she whispered to Louise, "It's all guesswork. No one has anything useful to say."

As the paramedics prepared Bella for the ride to the hospital, Vicki, Nancy, and Louise gave their names and contact information to the sheriff's deputy. Nancy noticed Vicki taking long looks at the bystanders watching the action, then she waved at Nancy on her way to the parking lot. "I'm following her to the hospital," she said.

The sheriff's deputy told the bystanders to leave and continued to survey the scene. Nancy and Louise walked back to the building.

Louise took a seat in the lobby while Nancy knocked on Harry's door and walked into his office to alert him to the incident.

"But why?" Harry asked, tearing at his hair. "Why Bella of all people? What happened?"

"Bella has been spreading lies about the investigation and implying she knew who the killer was."

"Why would she do that?" asked Harry. "Didn't she have any idea how dangerous that could be?"

Nancy shrugged "They wanted to catch the killer, but he may have tried to kill her instead."

Had Bella discovered something suspicious in the basement? Was it an accident or had a thief or a murderer felt threatened and hit her on the head?

All You Want to Know About Bees

Did you know the stack of white boxes near the garden is a bee hive? It's managed by our own Louise Owens, beekeeper extraordinaire. She will talk about bees and their habits at the next meeting of the Master Gardeners. Everyone is invited to attend. The meeting will be held in Classroom A, Basement Level, on Tuesday at ten a.m. Louise assures us that her bees are industrious, healthy, and gentle. They won't bother you unless you bother them.

The Whisperwood Breeze,
Newsletter of Whisperwood
Retirement Village

Chapter 27

Nancy and Louise walked back to Nancy's apartment. "I hope Bella and Vicki are all right," said Nancy as she called Vicki for an update.

"She's got a concussion and a bunch of bruises," Vicki said, "but the doctor seems to think she'll be okay. She'll be here for a couple of days. Now I've got calls to make, but thank you for asking."

"This place is getting on my nerves," Louise said. "Let's round up George and Fitz and have lunch in that cafe in town."

Nancy gave Fitz an edited version of the news, conscious of possible hidden bugs, while Louise called George. They met in the parking lot and took Fitz's blue Cadillac down the mountain to the cafe on the outskirts of the small town a few miles from Whisperwood.

Cheery red-checked tablecloths adorned the tables with matching curtains on the large windows that looked out on the road. The 90s Club sometimes brought friends there for small, informal celebrations. Lunch today was not a celebration.

"Glad to see you folks," said the host, a tiny, matronly woman with a dimpled smile. Her name, Cindy, was embroidered in pink on her black top. "What's happening up there at Whisperwood?" she asked. "Sheriff's car went whizzing by a couple of hours ago."

Nancy hedged. "I'm sure he'll get it all cleared up."

The host grabbed four menus and led them to a table near the back wall.

They took their seats and perused the menu. The server arrived with glasses of water. She knew them all by sight. "You know what you want?" she asked.

"We do. Iced tea and BLT for me," said Nancy.

The others gave their orders just as quickly while Fitz surveyed the café from one side to the other. "I'm glad we're meeting here," he finally said. "Too many ears at Whisperwood, don't you think?"

"That Bella was asking for it," George grumbled. "She's lucky I didn't bash her head in myself." He looked up. "But I didn't."

"She scared somebody," said Louise. "And they tried to get rid of her."

"But who?" Nancy asked.

They all fell silent as they contemplated the question. The server brought their drinks.

"It must be someone we all know," Fitz said when she'd left. "Had Bella met Sterling?"

"Sure. He hung around with Simon, and Bella liked Simon," George snickered, "almost as much as she did me. She must have met Sterling."

"Probably," said Nancy, "but she was fishing, nosing around, and she probably picked up a bit of information dangerous to the killer and blabbed it to everyone."

"She could have tried blackmailing the killer," added Louise, "if she knew what she knew."

George placed his napkin on his lap. "Bella wasn't a bright dollar, and she was silly. She probably had no idea she was stomping into dangerous territory."

Fitz rapped on the table. "We need to talk to Vicki."

"She's at the hospital," Nancy said. "We should stop by there on our way back, but Vicki said Bella will be okay."

She fell silent when their sandwiches arrived. Conversation ceased until the server went on to other tables as more customers arrived. The hum of conversation in the cafe increased.

"Any word from that jeweler you visited?" asked Louise, setting her sandwich aside.

"Several of those diamonds could be identified by their laser tags," Nancy said. "We have to rely on the jeweler to try to find out who owned them. Then we have to figure out how Glinda got them."

"Piece of cake," Louise said sarcastically.

"What about Vicki?" asked Fitz.

"Bella's sister?" George shook his head. "She's level-headed, but she tried to protect Bella and didn't put stock into any of Bella's fanciful ideas. I don't see her harming her sister."

"If she didn't hurt Bella, which we're sure she didn't," put in Fitz, "then she probably didn't kill Alex either and knows nothing about the trunk."

Nancy shook her head. "I don't think we can make

any assumptions about this yet."

"But someone hit the woman," George protested.

"I agree because I didn't see anything there that would cause such an injury."

"My bet is on Simon," said Louise.

"He's a front runner, all right," agreed George.

"I don't know..." Nancy munched her sandwich thoughtfully. "We ought to be careful around any of our suspects and suspicious of anyone who seems too interested. That includes Vicki...and Bella, if she survives. She loves to be the center of attention and gossip."

"What are our next steps?" asked Louise. "I want to be doing something."

"We'll see what the jeweler in Charleston finds out about the diamonds," said Fitz.

"Ashley can keep letting us know what the sheriff's deputies are doing," added Nancy.

"I'll continue to monitor the cameras in the basement and tunnel room," said Fitz. "Nothing has happened there so far."

"I'll bet," said Louise. "The thief is staying far away from anything that could tie him to the murders."

"I'll be my charming self to Vicki and I guess I could visit Bella in the hospital, but I don't have to eat dinner with Vicki, do I?" George asked.

Nancy hid a smile as she saw Louise bite off a retort, but all she said was, "Suit yourself."

"By the way," said Fitz, "the Elmos are having a small memorial service for Alex in the chapel here."

"Good," said Nancy. "We can all go. Maybe we'll pick up some tidbit of information about him that will be useful. When is it?"

"I just happened to hear them making arrangements with Ashley for the use of the Chapel. Day after tomorrow. Ten a.m."

The server brought them their checks and hovered as if she had something to say.

Nancy looked up at her with an encouraging smile.

She twisted the apron in her hands. "You're the crime solvers at Whisperwood," she said haltingly.

"That's what they call us," said George.

"You know that man who was killed there? Alex something? He came here a few times. Once with the older couple who were his grandparents, but several other times with two other men, and I think they lived at Whisperwood."

"Would you know them if we showed you photos?" asked George.

"Probably," she said. "They mostly talked softly—couldn't hear what they said. Once they got into an argument, but it didn't last long."

"Thank you for this," Nancy said.

"We hope you catch the murderer," the server added, "before he kills again."

"Sterling and Simon, I'll bet, with Alex," said Louise. "They were an unholy trio, I'd say."

"They keep popping up," said Fitz. "Alex and Sterling wouldn't have known about the tunnel room, though. Simon has been at Whisperwood for years, even before Glinda's murder. He knew all about the tunnels and might have seen the potential for that tunnel room himself. All he had to do was find a way to open and close the fake door, keep the steps already in place, and pay off a few workers to make sure the room wasn't filled in."

George raised an eyebrow. "You think Simon used that room."

Fitz frowned at him. "Who else?" he asked.

Patronize Your Local Merchants

The merchants in town and around the area are pleased to have Whisperwood Retirement Village in their neighborhood and welcome Whisperwood residents to their stores. When you buy in the area, be sure to ask for the Whisperwood discount.

The Whisperwood Breeze,
Newsletter of Whisperwood
Retirement Village

Chapter 28

Caroline brought Cleo over the next morning for a "play date," and then left to make a trip into town. The two cats were happily batting a paper wad around the living room. Nancy watched them over her teacup, but then she heard a rap on the door.

Vicki stood outside, both hands jammed into the pockets of her jeans. "May I come in?"

"Of course." She ushered Vicki into the living room. "How is Bella?"

"She has a concussion, bruises, and big bump on her head, but she'll be all right."

"I'm glad to hear that. Did you find out who attacked her?"

Vicki shook her head. "She didn't see or remember anything."

"Too bad. Have a seat. Would you like some tea?"

Vicki sat on the couch. "Thank you. Is Malone the big cat? I've heard so much about him. He doesn't seem mean at all." She looked shattered and not at all the efficient, capable person she had been.

Nancy explained the play date. "Cleo's the little

female. They are pals."

"How nice," Vicki said absently.

She watched the cats as Nancy prepared a tray with teacups, sugar, lemon, and crisp gingerbread cookies. She brought the tray out, poured tea, and handed a cup to Vicki.

"We are so sorry Bella got hurt," Nancy began.

"Thank you," Vicki said and sipped the tea, then put the cup aside. She leaned forward. "I want your help."

"Of course," Nancy said. "Whatever I can do…"

"I mean the 90s Club." She stared at Nancy intently. "Everyone here knows of its reputation for solving crimes. Someone tried to kill my sister."

"The sheriff's investigator is on the job," Nancy said. "He has interviewed me and Louise and others at Whisperwood."

"He seems competent," said Vicki. "He's following the procedures, but he doesn't know any of us. The two murder victims had records, but they didn't kill themselves, did they?" She stood and paced back and forth. "I haven't seen any suspicious characters around, and everyone else, including you and Fitz, are clean, but someone here—here at Whisperwood, I mean—murdered those two men and tried to kill my sister. You know the people here. Who would do this?

Nancy saw the anguish in her eyes. "We are working on it," Nancy said cautiously.

"Whatever you know, you need to tell the sheriff's investigator," Vicki said. "He has the resources and skills to put everything together."

"Of course," said Nancy. She was through confronting murderers herself. "We know the Elmos and we knew Glinda Spencer, whose steamer trunk seems to be at the heart of these murders. Why do you think someone tried to kill your sister?"

Vicki drummed her fingers on the side table for a moment, obviously thinking hard.

Was she making up a plausible story? Nancy sat back and waited.

"It's complicated," Vicki said at last.

"Start with why you moved here."

Vicki sighed. "First, you need to know my sister trained as an actress. She was a beauty in her day. She had even met Glinda when she worked briefly in Anchorage and Fairbanks at venues catering to the cruise ships and tourists. In the winter, she worked in Hawaii or Arizona and sometimes Bella got a job in a film so she lived in Hollywood. She never made it big, but people liked her, and she had fans. Until..." Vicki's voice turned bitter, "we retired and moved here."

"Do you know anyone who had a grudge against Bella?" Nancy asked.

Vicki shrugged. "Show business. Bella didn't get along with Glinda when they met in Alaska, but then, no one did." Vicki shrugged. "Anyway, she was dead long before we came here. I can't think of anyone else." She sighed. "I guess I should tell you..."

"What?" Nancy asked.

"Bella had heard the show brussiness gossip when she was in Alaska. Something about how Glinda had hidden a stash of coins or diamonds or some such somewhere. Common gossip in the business. Probably made up stories, totally fabricated, but we speculated.

We were planning on moving here anyway since we grew up in West Virginia, our family's here, and we thought it would be fun to look for Glinda's treasure."

"This was common knowledge?" Nancy asked. "All of you knew about it?"

"Those of us who worked with her did, like Bella. I doubt if Barbara or Don Elmo knew. I heard they didn't have much to do with Glinda. Alex must have learned about it from Sterling. Simon had known them in Alaska, but not well. I don't think he'd heard about it. Alex and Sterling told everyone they were looking for Glinda's trunk. Even Bella was curious about it. But someone else, the murderer, also knows about the trunk."

"Bella implied she knew something about the murders and she learned it from George," Nancy said. "Why would she say something like that? George didn't tell her anything."

Vicki sighed. "Her vanity talking. She liked to aggrandize herself. I had to rein her in most of the time, but I wasn't quick enough to see what she was doing. Whatever her faults, she doesn't deserve to be murdered. She must have found out something."

Nancy glanced at her watch. Caroline should be back to pick up Cleo in a few minutes, and then she was meeting Fitz for lunch at the Pub. As these thoughts crossed her mind, she heard a rap at the door.

"That's my neighbor here to pick up her kitty," Nancy said, rising.

Vicki stood, too. "Time for me to go," she said.

"Thank you for telling me about you and Bella. We'll do what we can," said Nancy. Then because she didn't know Vicki well and how she might repeat this conversation, she added, "The sheriff's investigator is on the job. We are only an adjunct to his efforts."

Sure," said Vicki and winked. "I know all that."

She left as Caroline entered, looking for Cleo who was hiding behind the couch. Malone sat on the windowsill watching. Caroline coaxed Cleo to come out and as Cleo crept forward, Caroline grabbed her. "Thanks, Nancy. Did they play together all right?"

Nancy smiled. "They seem to like each other. Bring Cleo over any time we're here."

Caroline glanced doubtfully at Malone. "I'd like to reciprocate, but..."

"Don't worry. Malone will be better off here, and we're used to him."

***

Fitz was waiting for Nancy in the Pub when she arrived. "I talked to Ashley before I got here," he said. She reports the sheriff's investigators are looking carefully into Vicki and Bella's background and any Alaska connection. She thinks Simon is their prime suspect."

Nancy nodded. "He would be mine, too, except that he knew Glinda and as far as I know, has never shown an interest in her trunk. By the way, Vicki says everyone who knew Glinda thought she had a stash hidden away somewhere. That is, everyone except for Simon."

Fitz shook his head. "I don't see Vicki killing her sister, do you?"

Nancy agreed. "She has asked us to help find Bella's attacker."

"We're on it," said Fitz.

"We've already ruled out Barbara and Don," added Nancy. "They wouldn't kill their grandson, and I can't believe two killers are running around Whisperwood."

***

After lunch, Nancy opened her laptop to check her e-mail. She found a message from Tom Taylor with a forwarded message from a diamond lab in New York City.

She called out to Fitz. "Come over here. We've got a response." She didn't say more, conscious of possible hidden bugs nearby.

Fitz looked over her shoulder while she opened the email and clicked on the forwarded message. She quickly perused the diamond specifications to read the information given about the 1.75-carat colorless, perfect diamond. According to the company records, the diamond was inscribed by a company in Winnipeg, Canada, which sold it to a LaDianne Richards, also of Winnipeg. Nancy glanced at Fitz. He circled his hand to signal her to continue.

She googled LaDianne Richards and found her website and Facebook page. The website featured a photo of a glamorous young African-American woman with a brief bio and a promotional blurb. Across the top was a banner noting that she was on a long-needed vacation and break from show business. An email address and number for her agent were provided.

Nancy studied the photo, imagining the woman with hair drawn back into a chignon and wearing glasses and business clothes. A match for Violet Velois. Interesting, but was she a killer?

Nancy picked up her cell phone and she and Fitz left the apartment to step out to the gardens through the side exit door in the hall.

She called Tom Taylor and asked him to send La-Dianne an email, asking if she still had the diamond or had disposed of it, claiming that he had a possible buyer for it.

"If this wasn't part of the murder investigation I've read about in the newspapers," Taylor told Nancy, "I'd be reluctant to play a part in this deception."

"I would ask her myself, but since you are the one who received the information from the lab, you should be the one to pursue it," said Nancy.

"Yes, they released that information to me because I'm in the trade," said Taylor.

Nancy nodded. "We know she still doesn't have the diamond. It may have been stolen or sold. How did Glinda get hold of it? Did she buy it? Steal it? If LaDianne sold it to Glinda, we'll know Glinda came by it legitimately. That might indicate the other gemstones were also legitimately purchased."

"LaDianne could have sold it to someone else," said Taylor.

"Could you help us clarify this?"

"I'll try," Taylor said. "I'll let you know what happens."

Nancy understood his reluctance, but they needed to learn where the gemstones came from and LaDianne's diamond was the best lead they had so far.

"Meanwhile, we'll hope to hear from LaDianne Richards aka Violet Velois."

Nancy turned to Fitz, standing beside her. "What's next?" she asked. "I'm stumped."

"Let's recap," Fitz said. "Alex Elmo, a convicted felon, was visiting his grandparents here and was found shot against one of the outbuildings on the grounds. He was looking for Glinda's trunk."

"Wait," said Nancy. "We need to begin back when Glinda was murdered over a year ago. We thought it was because she had discovered incriminating evidence against the previous administration. Could there have been another reason? We know she was a petty thief and blackmailer."

Fitz led Nancy to an isolated bench along the path. "Glinda's sister Barbara and her husband Don Elmo showed no interest in Glinda's trunk, which we now know held a fortune in gemstones."

"The same with Glinda's sons, Cary and Grant. The trunk was discarded."

"More than a year later," Fitz continued, "Glinda's great-nephew Alex, a convicted felon, and her ex-husband and business manager, Sterling Cooper, came here to look for Glinda's trunk. Shortly after he arrived, Alex was shot and killed next to one of Whisperwood's outbuildings."

"No one knew what happened to Glinda's trunk," Nancy added, "but we found it with other items in the tunnel under the basement. Someone had hidden thousands of dollars worth of precious gems inside the trunk."

"We're assuming Glinda did that, but what if someone else did it after Glinda died?" said Fitz. "If Glinda did it, where did she get the gems? Who hid them in the trunk? Who hid the trunk in the tunnel?"

"And who killed Alex Elmo?"

"We have three victims," said Fitz. "Who killed Sterling Cooper and who attacked Bella? Why?"

"Alex, Sterling, Bella, and Simon had all known Glinda. Glinda moved to Whisperwood to be close to her sons, living in Morgantown, West Virginia. The others had their reasons for coming here, but what if their real reasons all had to do with the hidden gemstones?"

"And what if someone else here knew Glinda? They could also be searching for the trunk. If one of the others recognized that person, would it lead to murder?"

"It would probably be someone very new to Whisperwood who had also just learned of Glinda's death."

Fitz chuckled. "Reminds me of the adage, 'Follow the money.'"

"We found the trunk and discovered it hid precious gemstones, and we've set up hidden cameras to find out who stored it and other stolen items in the basement. Are the thief and the murderer the same person?"

"We found out Alex and Sterling have criminal records," added Fitz.

Nancy nodded. "Ashley is our mole in the sheriff's office."

"We contacted Tom Taylor and enlisted his aid in appraising the gems and in tracing the diamonds hidden in Glinda's trunk," said Fitz.

"I'll check my email on my phone," said Nancy, "to see if there's another response from him." A quick check showed no response yet. She turned around and looked at Fitz. "I want to find out what happened that both Alex and Sterling came to Whisperwood at the same time to find Glinda's trunk. What did they hear? Who from? Somebody must have spread the news that her trunk was worth a fortune."

"And that she had died here at Whisperwood," said Fitz. "I suppose some news takes a long time to get passed around."

"Glinda got those stones from somewhere. Probably from a jeweler. We need to take a closer look at Simon, who is a retired jeweler. He knew all of those people from Alaska, including Glinda."

"You're right. We need to talk to Simon," said Fitz. "He would be the logical one to supply Glinda with gemstones."

"And knowing how he operates, they could have been stolen."

"We need to chat. I'll call him," said Nancy. "We'll take him to dinner. Should we meet him in town or ask him to join us in the dining room here?"

Fitz thought a moment before replying. "He might feel safer away from here and with fewer people. How about that new restaurant in town, the Firestone Inn?"

Nancy grinned. "Excellent. People have been talking about how good their food is. Simon will probably be delighted to eat at a gourmet restaurant for a change."

"We'll ply him with good food and liquor," Fitz said, rubbing his hands together. "And us, too."

Nancy grinned. "He'll be putty in our hands."

**Notice to Residents
July 4th Picnic, Barbeque,
and Fireworks**

Whisperwood's annual 4th of July picnic and barbeque is coming up soon. If you'd like to invite friends or family to join you in this celebration, please fill out the form attached and give it to Ashley at the reception desk. Cost for guests is $15 for adults and $10 for children under age 12. Residents and children under 6 are free. The fireworks show begins at nine p.m. and will be supervised by our local volunteer firefighters.

The Whisperwood Breeze,
Newsletter of the Whisperwood
Retirement Village

Chapter 29

Nancy made a quick call to Louise to explain their absence at dinner that night, and she and Fitz waited in the lobby for Simon to join them. Then they drove down the mountain in Fitz's Cadillac to the historic district for the Firestone Inn.

Simon's eyes widened as he saw the colonial brick front and artificial torches on each side of the entrance. "This looks nice," he breathed. "I got to tell you, I'm mighty tired of the standard stuff they serve in the dining room."

"We've been wanting to try this place," said Nancy. "It comes highly recommended. We're pleased you could join us as our guest."

"Excellent," Simon said, straightening his jacket and bow tie. "This is the kind of place I'm used to, but I can't imagine what you expect of me."

They were soon seated at a table with fresh flowers and a lanterned candle as the centerpiece. Fitz opened the wine list. A sommelier arrived. "May I take your drinks order?" he asked.

Simon sat back, a pleased and smug look on his

face. "I'd like a whiskey on the rocks," he said

Fitz nodded and ordered cabernet sauvignon for Nancy and himself. They all perused the menu and allowed Simon to order first. "I'll have that roque-fort-crusted filet mignon," he told the server. He turned to Fitz. "I'll tell you, I miss the high-in restaurants I used to frequent in Chicago and New York. This is a rare treat."

Fitz and Nancy both ordered the grilled New York steak. As the server left, the sommelier returned with their drinks. Simon took a long sip with closed eyes and a slight smile. Then he opened his eyes. "Now that's more like it," he said.

"How is everything going for you?" asked Fitz to get the ball rolling.

"Guess I've got to pay for my supper," said Simon. "Is that it?"

"You and Sterling Cooper seemed to know each other," Nancy began. "Tell us about Sterling."

"Sure. I knew Sterling. Spend any time in those tourist towns in Alaska, and you get to know everybody who lives there. Glinda, his wife, sang in the saloons lining the streets, and he drove the tourist buses on excursions into the wilderness, then dropped them off at the saloons with coupons for half-price drinks. From what I could see, he spent his off time drinking with the tourists himself."

"How long were he and Glinda married?" asked Fitz.

"Don't know. A few years. She saw through him pretty quick, but he was good at driving customers into the saloons, which helped Glinda keep her job, so she kept him around for a while until she realized he was drinking up her salary. She kicked him out fast then, but by that time she was getting ready to retire anyway."

Nancy watched Simon for any signs that might reveal nuances in what he said, but the flickering candle in the dim light, however romantic, prevented close observation. She asked a question instead. "Why do you think he was murdered?"

Simon sat back, affronted. "Why was Alex murdered? Or Sterling for that matter. I don't know. And I can't figure out who did it, either, in case that's your next question."

"But why? What was everyone after?" asked Fitz coolly, appraising Simon across the table. "What was in Glinda's trunk that drew Alex and Sterling? Like them, you were one of those who knew Glinda in Alaska. That's the key to the murders."

Simon flinched. "Don't ask me. Sentimental value?"

"We've been looking for that trunk," said Nancy. "No luck. I guess you are, too."

"It's probably long gone in the local dump. Piece of junk." He finished his dinner and declined dessert. "You can take me home now," he said, laying aside his napkin and pushing his chair back. "You've upset my stomach, and I've told you all I know, which is next to nothing."

Oh, I doubt that, Nancy thought.

They drove back to Whisperwood in silence. Nancy was not pleased with her performance. They had gotten nothing out of Simon and succeeded only in making him extremely suspicious of them and their motives and more nervous than he usually was. She wondered what they should do next.

Fitz drove to the front door. Simon left the car and strode to the entrance without a look back. Fitz drove on.

"Maybe we'll hear from Tom Taylor tomorrow," Fitz said, driving into Whisperwood's parking area. It was after nine. They greeted the night security guard in the lobby and walked down the hall. Nobody lurked. All was quiet. As they approached Nancy's apartment, she noticed a track of bloodstains and tiny bits of flesh on the rug in front of her door. Fitz tried the door. It was closed but not locked.

They entered the apartment to find the place a shambles. A couch pillow had been shredded and bits of foam rubber were scattered across the rug. A lamp was overturned, a vase broken, and papers were scattered on the dining room table. Only Malone was calm and unruffled, gently licking his paw from a perch on the back of the couch.

Fitz went immediately to Malone and petted him, crooning "Good kitty, good kitty." Nancy brought him a treat. "He's a good watch cat," Nancy said, examining his paws. Signs of blood appeared between the paws and under the nails.

"I don't think anything was taken, but what were they looking for?" Fitz cast his eyes around the room. "They tried to get into your computer." He nodded at the laptop, open on the table.

"Password protected," said Nancy. "Thank goodness Louise took our lists, and I didn't print out my notes. No hard copies anywhere."

"The gems are under lock and key," added Fitz. "I had my phone with me, so they couldn't tap into that."

"Whoever broke in will have scratches on their arms and face," said Nancy. "We'll keep a lookout."

"I'll pick up blood stain samples from Malone's paws for DNA testing. We can find out who did this and maybe it will be the murderer." Fitz brought several empty pill bottles and some cotton swabs from the kitchen. "Help me swab Malone's paws," he said.

Together, they picked up blood samples from Malone, who preened with all this attention.

"Somebody saw we weren't in the dining room tonight," Nancy said as they worked. They thought we'd gone out, and they'd have a clear field for snooping. Tomorrow I'll call the sheriff about this and give him the DNA sample."

"Set up your table in the lobby, too. You'll be able to watch people come in and out. Look for cat scratches, heavy make-up, or long sleeves in this summer weather. Whoever it was thought Malone was an ordinary house cat."

"I doubt that. Everyone who lives here knows how ferocious Malone can be," Nancy said. "Why would they think they could handle him?"

Pet Park Comes to Whisperwood
Responding to requests from numerous dog owners, Whisperwood is planning a dog park for our canine friends. The area will comprise close to an acre and will be placed next to the tennis courts. Fencing

in this area has already begun, and the park should be available for doggie use by September.

The Whisperwood Breeze,
Newsletter of Whisperwood
Retirement Village

Chapter 30

The first thing Nancy did, even before breakfast, was check her email, but she found nothing from Taylor. After breakfast, she reported the break-in to the sheriff's office, and they told her an investigator would be out later that morning. She photographed the damage in the apartment, ate her breakfast, and took her laptop to the lobby to set up shop. Fitz stayed home to wait for the sheriff's investigator.

As an extra reward for Malone, she called Caroline to invite Cleo for a play date. Caroline was long answering the phone and declined the offer.

"Just not feeling well," she said.

Louise came by as usual in her white beekeeper's suit, heading out to check on her hive. George wandered into the lobby and sat in an armchair next to her table. "Thought I'd help," he said "Heard about the break-in."

"We know it couldn't have been Sterling," said Nancy, "or even Simon since he was with us. I don't think Vicki would have left such a mess except that whoever broke in didn't reckon on Malone."

George shuddered. "I wouldn't ever want to tangle with Malone. He scares me."

"He's not for everyone," Nancy acknowledged. "That leaves Barbara and Don Elmo."

"There might be an "X" in the woodpile," said George. "Someone we haven't thought of yet."

"Could be." Nancy nodded. Three women bustled by, nodding at Nancy and George as they walked past and out the front door. They wore short-sleeved summer dresses. Arms and faces showed no scratches.

Then Violet Velois wandered out of her office and headed to the coffee bar. She wore slacks and a long-sleeved blouse. Nancy studied her ensemble but could see nothing suspicious. The air conditioning could be quite cold in the executive offices.

On her way back, coffee cup in hand, Violet stopped to chat. "I hear you and your friends are investigating the murders," she said. "Wish I could help."

"Keep your eyes and ears open," said George.

"I do, being the new kid on the block," Violet said. "I don't know anything about the murders, but I did meet Glinda Spencer once," she said. "I hear you think it's all about her brassbound antique trunk?"

"When did you meet Glinda?" asked Nancy, caught by surprise.

"I was an entertainer, too, you know," Violet said. "Had a summer gig on a cruise ship in Alaska. Spent a few extra days in Anchorage and went to see her show. They called her 'The Singing Canary.' She did have a good voice."

George groaned. "Yeah, we know."

Violet shrugged. "A mutual friend introduced us, and we went out to supper after she finished her sets.

Can't say I was impressed, but a squirrely little man who followed her around told me on the sly that she was a very wealthy woman. Whatever. She let the rest of us pick up her tab."

Nancy thought the squirrely little man was probably Sterling Cooper, acting as Glinda's manager. Nancy listened for acrimony, jealousy, or other negative emotions about Glinda from Violet, but couldn't detect anything that would hint at any kind of agenda.

"How did you hear about the trunk?" asked Nancy.

"Harry kept asking people about it, then he stopped, so I guess he found it." Violet waved her cup. "Got to get back to work," she said and returned to her office.

"That was interesting," said George. "Someone else who knew Glinda. Never suspected that."

Nancy checked her watch. After eleven a.m. She closed up her laptop. "I've got a better idea," she said.

"So have I," said George. "Let's pay a visit to the suspects."

Nancy grinned at George. "Great minds think alike. Wait here while I put the laptop in my apartment."

When she returned, George asked, "What's the reason for our visit?"

"Don't worry, I have one," said Nancy. "We'll say we heard a loud ruckus last night and with all the goings on, thought we'd better check on people connected in any way with Glinda to make sure they're all right."

George scratched his chin. "Yeah, that oughta

work. Maybe. I guess."

No one answered the door at Vicki's place. Nancy stared at the door, chewing her lip. "We can't draw any conclusions," she said. "Vicki's probably at the hospital. She doesn't have to be cowering inside with face and arms full of Malone's scratches and bites."

"We'll see her at dinner," George said.

Barbara opened the door when they knocked, but showed no signs of a Malone attack. "Don went to town," she told them. "We didn't hear any ruckus."

Simon Smythe didn't answer their knock but, of course, he'd been with Nancy and Fitz at dinner during the break-in.

"What a bunch of gadabouts," George said.

"Frustrating," Nancy agreed. "We'll have to watch for them at dinner."

"Did you pick up the blood samples?" George asked. "Call the sheriff?"

They had returned to the lobby. Nancy stopped at the coffee bar and poured out a cup for George and one for herself. "Let's sit here a while," she said, taking an armchair near the wall. George took the adjacent one.

"Fitz is waiting for the sheriff's investigator to show up," said Nancy. "We've got the blood samples, but analyzing the DNA will take weeks if not months."

George sipped his tea. "So what then? Seems like we're stymied."

"I'm waiting for a reply from the jeweler in Charleston. We're trying to track down where Glinda got the gemstones."

"We're assuming the murderer and the thief are the same," George said.

Nancy lifted an eyebrow. "Maybe, but now we might be talking about two thieves, the one who hid his stash in the tunnel room and the one who broke into my apartment. They might not be the same person. One, both, or neither could be the murderer."

"Hoo boy." George sighed and stood. "Thanks for an instructive morning, Nancy. Now I think I'll go home and google gemstone thefts in Alaska and Canada. Might come up with something."

Nancy refilled her cup and strolled to her apartment. Maybe there would be a message from Taylor in her email.

As she approached, she could hear Malone complaining. Fitz must have locked him in the bedroom while the investigator was there.

"Been and gone," Fitz said. "I told him the little information I had, but he saw the mess and the bloodstains and asked me to close Malone in the bedroom. Lieutenant Cal Madding. Here's his card." Fitz handed Nancy a business card.

"What about a DNA test on the bloodstains?" Nancy asked.

Fitz shrugged. "Since nothing was stolen and the break-in was probably not related to the murder—his words, not mine—the sheriff's office probably won't want to spend the money for DNA testing."

"So if we want DNA testing done, we'll have to order it ourselves from a private lab."

"Correct." Fitz walked over to Nancy and gave her a kiss and a hug. "Who said solving crimes is easy? Anyway, I vote for looking for Malone's marks on the thief first. Any luck there?"

Nancy shook her head. "Nobody showed up in the lobby except George, so we visited each of our prime suspects and only found one willing to answer the door. Barbara. No wounds were visible.

"Could makeup hide them?"

Nancy shrugged. "I suppose so, but we'd notice heavy make-up. They could wear slacks, shirts, gloves, whatever worked, to hide the scratches." She opened her laptop and checked the emails. Nothing from Tom Taylor.

"Let's get lunch in the Pub," said Fitz. By this time, Malone's complaints had become so loud and aggrieved that Fitz let him out of the bedroom. "Sorry, old guy. You're a very good cat."

Nancy gave him a treat, and they left for the Pub leaving Malone again in charge. As Nancy reminded Fitz, he was quite a capable cat.

Open Mic Night at Whisperwood
Whisperwood has talent! Poets, writers, musicians—we'll lend you our ears. Sign up to read your poetry, essay, or other work or to play your musical instrument. The event will be held August 8 at 7 p.m. in the auditorium. Sign up now with Violet Velois, Life Enrichment Director.
The Whisperwood Breeze,
Newsletter of Whisperwood
Retirement Village.

Chapter 31

Nancy and Fitz both ordered BLTs and iced teas as usual at the Pub Bar and took seats at a table by the window.

"Have you checked your phone yet?" Nancy asked in a low voice.

"I'll do it now." Fitz took out his phone and checked both cameras. The one in the hall had filmed people going to and from the classrooms, but no one showed an interest in the end wall. The other camera, inside the tunnel room, had a dark screen. "Nothing," he said.

"We need to create a reason for the thief to want to check the tunnel room," Nancy said. "He doesn't know we've taken his stash out of there. He has to want to check."

"It has to be subtle enough so he doesn't suspect a trap." Fitz looked up as the server delivered their food.

"We need a brainstorming session with the 90s Club," Nancy said. "This afternoon if we can get everyone together."

Fitz called George and Louise. "This afternoon,

Two p.m., Louise's apartment," he said to Nancy as he tucked his phone away.

***

Louise set the teapot, four cups, and a bowl of sugar and artificial sweetener packets on the coffee table in her living room. "The meeting is called to order," she said.

Nancy took the lead. "We need some brainstorming," she said. "How can we get the thief to check the tunnel room without suspecting a trap?"

"So the camera hasn't captured anyone going down there?" asked George.

Fitz shook his head. "As long as he thinks his stash is secure, why would he?"

"Unless he had a buyer for one of the items," added Louise as she poured tea into the cups. "Was there anything of Glinda's in the stash we found other than the jewels that someone would pay big money for?"

"Does it have to be Glinda's?" asked George.

"He stole from the living, too," Nancy said. "We don't want to pick an item that a resident here would claim."

"I guess that's right," conceded George. "You made a list, didn't you? Let's go through it."

"Wait a minute," said Fitz. "I have a better idea."

The other three turned to him expectantly.

"We'll get Harry to announce that the maintenance staff have found an unusual outflow of water from underneath the building. They think groundwater seeped into the filled-in tunnels and formed a stream."

"Great idea," George said. "Harry can reassure the residents that this will not affect the building, but if residents notice an outflow of water from under the building, they are not to be alarmed. The water is being monitored."

Nancy high-fived George. "Excellent. The thief will want to check to make sure his stash is high and dry."

"Yeah, that should get us a photo of the thief," said Louise, "but the thief may not be the murderer."

Fitz took a sip of tea and nodded. "We think the murders were connected with the gemstones in Glinda's trunk. The thief had the trunk but might not have known about the gems. The first victim, Alex, was searching for it. The second victim—that's Sterling—was also looking for it and might have recognized someone here from the past. Bella could have been attacked because she stumbled onto the murderer's identity."

"She's still in bad shape," said Nancy. "I heard Vicki insisted on a guard at Bella's room. Vicki's spending most of the day with her."

George leaned back in his chair with arms folded. "Seems like there has to be a connection."

Nancy rose. "Shall we go talk to Harry?"

They trooped down the hall to Harry's office.

"Here comes the posse," Ashley said as the 90s Club passed her and entered the executive suite. Harry's secretary, out-numbered, waved them in. Violet Velois looked on. Nancy tapped on Harry's door and the four walked into his office.

Harry looked up, sighed, and sat back. "To what do I owe the pleasure?"

Conscious of the interested eyes and ears of the

staff, Nancy closed the office door.

Fitz explained about the camera set up in the tunnel room. "So," he summed up, "we need a reason for the thief to go down there and get his picture taken."

"Why would he do that?" Harry asked.

George explained his idea. Harry pursed his lips and nodded. "That will work," he said. "I'll put a notice in the residents' inboxes this afternoon."

"Tell Ashley to reassure residents who ask her about this, " Nancy said. "There won't be any damage to the building or inconvenience to them at all. We don't want a panic."

Harry nodded. "Sure. I've got enough on my hands. If this will catch the killer, go for it."

"Hold on there," said George. "This may not be the killer, just a thief."

"Whatever," said Harry, waving them out.

URGENT TO ALL RESIDENTS
Maintenance staff have noticed an unusual outflow of water from under the building coming from the underground tunnels. These tunnels have been filled and barricaded, and present no danger to Whisperwood residents. This outflow of water on the grounds is being monitored and will be corrected immediately.

Harry Doyle, Administrator

Chapter 32

Later that afternoon, Nancy opened her email hoping for a response from Tom Taylor, and this time she wasn't disappointed. She pulled Fitz over. "I got an answer from Tom!'

"What does he say, Luv?" asked Fitz.

They both read the message without speaking.

"I contacted LaDianne Richards and introduced myself," Tom wrote, "but she at first disclaimed all knowledge of such a diamond. I asked if she knew a Glinda Spencer, and she didn't respond for a long while. Then she asked how I knew Glinda. I told her she had been murdered with the diamond in her possession. Then I asked if Nancy could call her, saying we were trying to track down the rightful owner of the diamond."

Nancy looked at Fitz. "She said it was okay if I called."

"Hmmm," muttered Fitz. "We'll need a strategy to get what we want out of LaDianne."

"I'm calling Tom right now," said Nancy and picked up the cell phone.

After the usual pleasantries, Nancy came to the

point. "How did Dianne react to news of the diamond? How did she feel about Glinda? What were your impressions of her?"

"Let me get my thoughts together," Taylor said.

Nancy waited.

Finally, Tom spoke, hesitantly at first. "You want my impressions? I'd say she sounded suspicious and a little frightened. She didn't know who I was and why I was calling. Her diamond was long gone. She said she sold it to Glinda while she was appearing in Anchorage. I don't think she liked or respected Glinda much. Those are just my impressions. I might be off base. I was out of my depth in that conversation, I'm afraid, but I have her phone number here so you can call her yourself.

Nancy wrote down the number even though she recognized it and thanked Taylor.

"Let me know what happens," said Tom.

"You bet." Nancy hung up the phone, turned to Fitz, and signaled to him that she was stepping out of the building again. She whispered, "I'm going to call LaDianne, and I think I know how to play it."

Outside on the path, she made the call. A woman answered. "Is this LaDianne Richards?" Nancy asked.

"Who is calling," responded a familiar cool voice.

Nancy introduced herself. "Tom Taylor, the jeweler, told me you said I could call."

"You're Nancy Dickenson?" The voice now sounded amused. "You want to know about the diamond?"

"That's right. We found it among the possessions of a woman known to be a thief and a blackmailer."

Nancy saw Fitz recoil at the strong words. "We think she stole the gems we found in an item she had owned, including the diamond that you had lasered."

There was a long silence. "I told Mr. Taylor I gave Glinda Spencer the diamond. I presume that's who you mean." The words were tentative as if trying out the idea.

"Did you sell it or any other gems to her?" Nancy asked.

"I don't have to explain myself to you." The voice sounded irritated. "But Glinda Spencer blackmailed people who thought they were her friends. She tried that on me and, yes, I gave her that diamond. I left the area and haven't heard from her since. Good riddance, I say."

"So you haven't seen her since?"

"No, ma'am. Mr. Taylor said she'd been murdered. I'm not surprised."

"Do you have any idea how she got the other gemstones?"

"What do you think?" LaDianne said. "Anyway, you live in a place loaded with women who have expensive jewelry. Glinda tainted every place and everything she had to do with." LaDianne hung up.

"Aha!" thought Nancy. Those last statements confirmed that LaDianne lived at Whisperwood as Violet Volois.

Nancy returned to her apartment and joined Fitz on the couch with Malone. She whispered to Fitz, "LaDianne confirmed that she gave or sold the diamond to Glinda and hinted it was blackmail."

"Glinda up to her usual tricks," said Fitz.

"LaDianne doesn't know that I found out she is our beloved life enrichment director, Violet."

Fitz put his arm around Nancy. "We need to talk with her about Glinda, Luv," Fitz said.

"Tomorrow. Meanwhile, we're no closer to finding the murderer." Nancy reached over to pet Malone, which he allowed.

Who's on the Line?

Is it your grandson? A friend? Relative? Or is it someone with a well-thought-out scheme to bilk you of thousands of dollars? Caller ID won't help you because those can be manipulated to show a local number or town while the caller may be in Nigeria. If you don't recognize the name or number, don't answer the phone. Let them leave a message and call back number if they are legitimate.

The Whisperwood Breeze,
Newsletter of Whisperwood
Retirement Village

Chapter 33

George arrived at dinner that night with a twin-kle and a grin, rubbing his hands together. "You won't believe what I found," he said after they were all seated.

The server arrived with water and a basket of rolls. George held up a hand to wait. After they gave the server their selections, George leaned forward.

"Out with it, George," Louise said, making circles with her hand.

"Wait a minute," said Fitz. He picked up the centerpiece and placed it on a window sill ten feet away.

George frowned at him and turned to Nancy and Louise. "I was surfing the net, nothing in particular in mind, but I happened to Google "Alaska Anchorage gemstones stolen" and came to a site describing unsolved crimes and this was a doozy. A wholesale gemstone distributor was robbed of thousands of dollars in loose gemstones even though he had put them in the hotel's room safe. It happened at a luxury hotel there, and—get this—the safe was robbed while the manager was in the cocktail lounge watching the local songstress, Glinda Spencer, aka "The Singing Canary.""

Fitz shook his head. "Glinda must have been involved. That lady was sure into gems. We found out she blackmailed LaDianne Richards out of a large diamond. Some of those other gems may also have come from blackmail or a robbery. She was a crook."

"Did the site mention anyone with the police who had charge of the case?" asked Nancy.

George nodded. "Yep. Wrote down his name."

"How about calling him tomorrow?" asked Nancy. "Find out if he can send us a list of the stolen gems. Tell him what we've got going on here."

Louise suddenly sat up. "Ask him if he knows anything about Alex Elmo or Sterling Cooper. I'll bet Sterling was the thief along with Glinda, maybe even Alex. They were all in cahoots."

"Hoo boy," said George. "We may be on our way to solving this case."

As they quietly high-fived each other, Nancy glanced at the other diners. The Elmos were watching them, noticed the high-fives, and stopped with forks in mid-air. Violet Velois sat at a table with other residents and occasionally cast amused glances their way. No one else paid them any attention.

"I'm concerned about what will happen if we contact the Anchorage police and give them any information about what we found," Fitz said, fiddling with his napkin.

"Why?" asked George.

"They'll call our local sheriff and want to know who we are." Fitz looked at the others with a quizzical smile. "We haven't told the local constabulary anything about the gemstones. What if they say we are obstructing their investigation?”

The four 90s Club members stared at each other.

“Oh, fiddle-faddle,” said Louise. “We’ll have to wait until we catch the thief, which should be in the next day or two.”

Nancy nodded. “Then we can call in the sheriff and tell him the story. After all, we don’t know for sure the trunk, gemstones, and murders are all connected.”

“Yeah,” George grumbled. “They’ll buy that.”

“Sounds like a good plan to me,” said Louise. “Anyone have a better idea? They keep telling us to stay out of their investigation, so we are.”

“Kind of,” said George.

“Anyway, whoever stole the gems in Anchorage may have nothing to do with two murders here in West Virginia,” said Nancy. “I would bet on Sterling or Alex for the theft in Anchorage, but they wouldn’t know anything about the tunnel room.”

“By the same token,” added Louise, “neither would Violet or Vicki. None of them moved here until the last month or so. They might have heard about the tunnels but not about the hidden door or the tunnel room.”

“Okay, then,” said George. “Full steam ahead.”

Nancy tackled her dinner with gusto, but she couldn’t stop thinking of Violet’s oddly amused expression. *What did that mean?*

As soon as she returned to the apartment after dinner, she opened her laptop and Googled LaDianne Richards, searching for any tidbit of information about the woman who found them so amusing.

Nancy located Violet"s Facebook page and her listing on LinkedIn but no recent entries were posted.

"I wonder why she gave up her musical career," Nancy said thoughtfully. "Other than her two websites, I've seen nothing recent about her."

Fitz was teasing Malone with a treat. "It's a tough life. She wanted to settle down," he said.

"I guess she thinks we don't know who she is," Nancy ventured. "She has been laughing at us. She looks so different here than in her website photo. She keeps her hair pulled back in a smooth chignon style. Hard to tell that LaDianne and Violet are the same person unless you're looking for it.

"She could have told us. Why didn't she?" asked Fitz.

"I guess she found it more fun this way. She must know we would find out eventually."

"Seems suspicious to me," Fitz said.

* * *

Harry followed through and had his secretary place a letter in every resident's inbox before dinner. Nancy retrieved hers as she and Fitz walked from the dining room to their apartment. Even Nancy thought Harry's message sounded credible and crossed her fingers that the camera in the tunnel room would record clear, recognizable images.

Louise and George headed to the elevators, but Louise whispered an admonition to Nancy. "Let us know immediately if you get those photos."

"Of course," said Nancy.

"I don't think the thief will try to enter until after nine when the corridor is empty," said Fitz, but he took a quick peek at his phone anyway.

"How would he try to get everything out of there?" Nancy asked.

Fitz shrugged. "No idea. How did he get everything down there in the first place?"

Nany flicked her hand. "He paid off the custodian and then killed him."

They stayed up until after midnight, hoping for images to appear on the cell camera. When none did, they went to bed.

At five a.m., Fitz's phone lit up, waking Nancy. She tapped on Fitz's shoulder. "We caught the fish," she said, holding up Fitz's phone which glowed.

Fitz blinked and stared at the images. "Simon." He watched as Simon Smythe, his face red with anger and disbelief, prowled the tunnel room.

"Yep. Simon," Nancy said. "I gave him a break the last time we caught him stealing from the residents, and he promised to desist."

"Not a man of his word," said Fitz.

"Look," said Nancy. "He has just discovered the camera." They watched as he reached up and then the picture went black.

"He yanked it away from the post, but we've got the video. He isn't happy."

"He knows we've got him," said Nancy. "He'll grab what he can and try to escape."

"There's nothing there to grab," reminded Fitz. "We've got to call the sheriff immediately," Fitz was already tapping in the numbers.

Nancy ran to the landline phone in the living room. "I'll let Louise and George know."

"Wait," said Fitz. "We don't know how Simon will react now. Tell them to be on their guard." He looked sternly at Nancy. "Us, too."

Notice to Residents
Routine Maintenance Scheduled

The water situation in the tunnels is being corrected. Whisperwood's Maintenance Engineers will now be conducting routine maintenance tasks in the next several weeks. They will contact you at least a day in advance if access to your apartment is needed, but most of the work will be conducted in the hallways and outside the building. We appreciate your cooperation.

Harry Doyle, Administrator

Chapter 34

The four 90s Club members stood under the portico watching the sun rise. They greeted Harry as he joined them. "So you got him?" he asked. "Let me see the video."

Fitz held his phone out to Harry. "Doggone it. You've got him, all right," said Harry. "Simon Smythe. He seemed like such a cultured gentleman."

The sheriff's investigator should be here any minute," said Nancy.

"What are you going to tell him?" asked Harry. "I don't want to be arrested for obstructing justice. We should have told him about the jewelry."

"Why?" asked Louise. "We were just trying to catch the thief, not a murderer. How do we know the gems and jewelry have anything to do with the murders? They could all belong to the residents. After all, Simon has stolen valuable items from residents before."

"What?' shrieked Harry. "I never heard about that."

"It's all right," put in Nancy. "After we caught him last year, he agreed to never steal from residents again. He did help us solve the murders then."

George frowned. "Pretty thin if you ask me," he grumbled.

"You got a better idea?" snarled Louise. "I think I hear a car."

"We have to stick with that story," said Fitz. "Even if Simon is the murderer, the murders and the thefts are two different problems."

"Let's not push that angle unless we have to," said Nancy. All of them were now watching the sheriff's car go through the gate, drive to the portico, and park in front of them. Lt. Harmason got out along with another officer.

"Where can we talk?" asked Harmason.

Harry led the group to a section of the dining room often used for private gatherings. Not even the staff were there this early. They took seats around a long table.

"Let me see this video," said Harmason.

Fitz opened his phone, made the selection, and handed the phone to Harmason. "We rigged up the camera inside the secret tunnel room in the basement."

"I thought the underground tunnels were closed and sealed," Harmason said, staring at Harry with a lifted eyebrow.

Harry nervously fiddled with his hands. He cleared his throat. "They were. That is, all but the section you see on the video. The board suggested we leave that section available in case we needed to get down there for some reason, but we did not put in a door so no one could have access. Never thought of it again. I was stunned when Nancy told me about the door."

Poor Harry, Nancy thought. His inexperience came through again and again.

Fitz cleared his throat. "Yet someone put in a secret door and camouflaged it so it wasn't visible unless you looked closely."

Harmason peered at the phone. "Who is the man caught in the video?"

"That is Simon Smythe," said Harry. "He has been here several years. He is a retired jeweler, I believe."

"That's right," said Nancy, "and also a thief. We discovered the tunnel room while searching for items the residents had reported missing. Simon used it to stash his stolen goods. We removed the items we found in the room, hid them in an unused apartment, and set a trap to find out who the thief was."

Harmason had been writing furiously in his notebook, but he looked up at Nancy. "Why didn't the residents report the thefts to the police?"

"The people here are elderly," Nancy said, "and some are quite forgetful. We all worry about dementia. Many reported the thefts to the office here and Harry has the list and descriptions of the lost items, but some didn't report thefts because they weren't sure they hadn't simply misplaced the items."

Harmason nodded. "I see."

Fitz cleared his throat. "We also found Glinda Spencer's brassbound trunk that the murder victims were looking for. When I took it apart to take it out of the tunnel room, I found a variety of gemstones, including emeralds, rubies, sapphires, and diamonds."

Harmason whistled.

Nancy held her breath. Here came the tricky part.

"Up till then, we hadn't connected these petty thefts with the murders."

Harmason watched her with a blank face. "Really," he said flatly.

"Yes, really," snapped Louise. "And just so you know, we made careful records of every item, including the rocks we found."

Fitz related to Harmason what they had done so far in attempting to find the owners of the gemstones and the stolen items, and how they decided to video the thief.

"He might be the murderer," added Fitz, "but he must know he's been identified and is probably planning a quick getaway."

"You're right," said Harmason. "We need to get to his apartment immediately." He got up and summoned the other officer and Fitz to follow him. "Bring your phone," he told Fitz. "You know where his apartment is and what he looks like."

Fitz squeezed Nancy's hand as he got up. "I'll report later," he whispered.

Nancy remained seated and watched Harmason and his posse head down the hall. "I should never have let him get away with it the first time," she said.

"Forget it," Louise said. "You gave him a break. He just wasn't smart enough to see it."

"Either that," said Nancy, "or desperate. Maybe he can't afford this place anymore. He has been here a long time, and Whisperwood is expensive."

"Hah!" said Louise. "We've got proof he's a thief and maybe a murderer. He won't have to worry about Whisperwood's fees for a long time."

Give Now to Whisperwood's Benevolent Fund Gala

This year's Gala will be a masquerade dinner and dance on Halloween, October 31, featuring our local dance band, The Buzzy King Band of Renown. Tickets go on sale Monday for this exciting, fun-filled annual event that benefits residents who have experienced a financial decline that threatens their living here. Let's help them and have a rollicking good time while we're doing it. Tickets may be bought at the reception desk or in the market store. Let's be generous this year.

The Whisperwood Breeze,
Newsletter of Whisperwood
Retirement Village

Chapter 35

Louise and George walked with Nancy to her apartment to wait for Fitz to return. By now, it was eight a.m. and the bakery in the little store off the lobby was open. Nancy bought a dozen muffins on her way.

"Breakfast," Louise said with a thumbs up to Nancy.

"I need some coffee," said George.

"Coming up." Nancy ambled into the kitchen to make the brew, setting the muffins on the table as she passed. Malone raised a lazy head from the bedroom but didn't bother to get up.

Louise took a sip of coffee and then demanded, "Who have we not considered yet?"

George swallowed a bite of muffin. "Seems a bit much to have both a thief and a murderer here."

"We knew Simon was a thief a year ago, but he was relatively benign," said Nancy. "He returned the items he stole and promised to stop."

"We were fools to believe he'd stop," grumbled George.

Nancy nodded. "Glinda was a thief, too, and a

petty blackmailer, but we're looking for a murderer, which seems to me to be a whole other class of criminal."

"The motive would have to be extremely compelling to resort to murder here," Louise said. "It wouldn't be like a hold-up at a convenience store where everyone had guns."

"I'd say a fortune in gems was a compelling motive," put in George.

"We know Alex Elmo was a low-life and a thief," Nancy said. "We don't know what else he could have been involved in."

George put down his cup. "We're all a bunch of nice people here, more or less," he said, "but nobody would want any of their dirty secrets revealed, would they? I could see Alex being a blackmailer."

Louise rapped on the table. "Blackmailers never give up. They keep asking for more. Drive their victims against the wall and still dig in."

"I need another muffin," said George, reaching for the box. "Brain food."

Louise snorted. "Sure."

"I don't see Bella as a blackmailer," Nancy said. "She must have threatened the murderer somehow."

"She found out who did it." George bit into a frosted orange muffin. "Delicious."

Nancy wandered to the window and saw Simon led out in handcuffs and helped into the sheriff's car. "The police have Simon," Nancy said. "Fitz should be back soon."

A few minutes later, Fitz entered followed by Caroline, holding her kitty. "She's driving me crazy,"

Caroline said. "Can she stay with you this morning?"

At that point, Malone ran into the living room and meowed up at Cleo, but this time Cleo seemed frightened. Her claws tore into Caroline's long sleeves. Her ears and fur seemed to stand erect. "I don't know what's gotten into her," said Caroline. "I guess this isn't a good idea today." she backed away from Malone and turned toward the door. Malone tried to follow, but Nancy held him back.

Then Caroline hesitated. "I came over to find out what's happening outside. Saw it through my window. Isn't that one of our residents being led out in handcuffs?"

"We were wondering about that, too," Nancy said.

"Do you think...?" Caroline said and stopped.

George finished her thought. "Maybe it's the murderer."

Caroline shuddered dramatically. "I certainly hope so." The cat growled as Caroline's grip on her tightened. "We're all scared to leave our apartments."

Fitz closed the door as Caroline left, trying to pull Cleo's claws out of her clothes.

Odd behavior, Nancy thought, but she was more interested in Fitz's report. "How did it go?" She asked.

"Simon's not happy." Fitz laughed. "Harmason expects us at the sheriff's office later today with a full accounting of what we found to sort this out. Simon will try to step away from this one since the stolen items had all been removed from the tunnel." He grimaced at the other three. "By us, if you remember."

Louise placed her hands on her hips and glared at Fitz in disbelief. "You mean he might walk because there weren't any stolen goods in the tunnel room?"

Fitz nodded. "Yep. Simon insists he was just curi-ous and happened to notice the hidden door."

Nancy laughed. "I kind of liked Simon. Maybe he'll get another free pass."

"But what about the murders?" George asked.

"Disclaims all knowledge," said Fitz. "I can't come up with a motive for him, can you? He says he didn't know about the gems."

They stared at each other glumly. Malone ran to the front door and clawed at it.

"I wonder what happened to Malone and Cleo?" said Louise. "Their romance seems to have turned sour."

"Seemed happy the last time they were together," Fitz said.

"Well, all right," Nancy said at last. "The sheriff might not have enough to charge him, but we know Simon is the thief, and we have his ill-gotten gains, so I think we should go about identifying the owners and returning their jewelry."

"Maybe Simon could help," Louise said with a laugh.

George arched an eyebrow. "Sure. That will work."

"Meanwhile," Louise said, "have we heard from the Anchorage police about the jewel theft there?"

Fitz took a sheet of paper out of his pocket and unfolded it. "Here's the list of the stolen articles they emailed to George. We can compare it with the list of articles we found. The Anchorage police also sent a copy to our local sheriff."

"I wonder what our sheriff thought," said Nancy. "He didn't know anything about the gemstones."

"The Anchorage police got curious when they received your request and contacted the sheriff here." Fitz laid the paper on the dining room table. "The sheriff told him 'a bunch of busybodies were muscling in where they don't belong.' His words, not mine." He grinned.

"He would be nowhere without us," said Louise.

"I guess we can expect another visit from Lt. Harmason before long," Nancy said.

"Now he knows what we've been up to," put in Fitz. "We talked early this morning when we confronted Simon. Don't expect thanks from him, though."

"But we still don't know who killed Alex and Sterling," added George.

"I don't think Simon murdered anyone," Nancy said thoughtfully.

"What about the custodian we think helped him with the hidden door?" asked Louise.

Nancy nodded. "His death is suspicious, but it could easily have been an accident."

"If I were Simon, I would have skedaddled as soon as I saw the camera," George said.

Louise shook her head. "I don't think it would be that easy. He has a lot of money tied up here, and if he had to resort to stealing, he might not have much in the bank. Where would he go without money?"

"If we take him off the list of murder suspects, who's left?" asked Nancy. "And is there someone we haven't thought of yet?"

"I took a look at the new arrivals to Whisperwood

during the week before Alex's murder," said Nancy. "Just curious, you know, but it occurred to me that something had to set events in motion and a new arrival might have been the catalyst."

"Whisperwood is always getting new people in," objected Louise. "Alex Elmo and Sterling Cooper, together or alone, could have been the catalyst."

"If Vicki's still a suspect, she and Bella arrived several weeks ago," added George.

Louise waved away George's suggestion. "I'll tell you the name of one person who showed up around the same time as Alex and Sterling," she said.

The others turned to her. "Who?" they asked.

"Miss Violet Velois, that's who," Louise said. "Our esteemed life enrichment director."

"Hmmm," said George. "Whisperwood's glamor gal. I don't mind seeing her around."

"I checked her references," Nancy said. "LaDianne Richards is her stage name."

"Wait," said Louise, "Isn't that ...?"

"Yep," said Nancy. "She's from Chicago and she owned one of the lasered diamonds in Glinda's trunk."

"So she must know about Glinda's collection of gemstones," George said. "Is she another person looking for Glinda's trunk?"

"Maybe she's on the run," George suggested.

"I didn't find Violet's name on any criminal databases," said Nancy.

Louise shook her head. "Doesn't smell right to me. She has herself lined up to do a program of songs for us under the name she gave us."

"What is a talented big city glamor puss like Violet doing in our pastoral setting?" asked George.

"Let's go ask her," said Nancy, glancing at her watch. "She should be in her office by now."

The foursome marched down to the executive offices and breezed past Ashley. Nancy rapped on Violet's door.

"Come in" was the soft response.

Nancy opened the door and a slight smile crossed Violet's face as she saw the foursome crowding through her doorway.

"To what do I owe the pleasure?" she asked.

This time, Fitz took the lead. "We know you're a glamorous and successful singer from Chicago whose stage name is LaDianne Richards," he began. "We're wondering why you chose a job here?"

Violet closed the folder she was perusing and folded her hands on top. "I don't know about glamorous or successful," she said, "but I got tired of the late nights, the pressure, that kind of life. Too precarious and too much stress. I didn't want to do it anymore."

"And," she said, "I knew Glinda Spencer used to live here. I didn't hear about her death until several weeks ago. I thought this might be the time to find out what she did with the diamonds she stole from me." She smiled. "Getting this job was a slam dunk, okay? I'm well qualified for it, and this is a beautiful place to live."

After a moment of stunned silence, Nancy cleared her throat and said, "You know we found at least one of your diamonds. It had a laser tag."

"It still belongs to me," Violet said. "How do I get it back and my other diamonds? I have appraisal documents for all my gems. I can prove they belong to me. Glinda stole them."

Fitz stepped forward. "We found gemstones hidden in an old trunk that had belonged to Glinda. One of them was the diamond Nancy mentioned. These gems have been listed and held in the safe in Harry's office. They'll be given to the sheriff's office to determine ownership. "

"I'll contact the sheriff immediately and place a claim." Violet picked up the phone and nodded at the four still standing at the doorway. "You got what you came for. You're all dismissed."

"But why didn't you report the theft to the sheriff?" asked Nancy. "Or confront Glinda?"

"Good questions," Violet said. "She blackmailed me, and I'm sure I wasn't the only victim. I knew she stole from others, but I had no proof, no idea where she might have hidden them, and I didn't want her to sue me for slander or expose my secrets. She didn't try to sell them or wear them, so I couldn't point them out and accuse her of theft with the documents to show I was the true owner."

"So she got away with it," said Louise. "That's our Glinda, all right."

"Thank you for seeing us." Nancy turned to leave. "You cleared up a few things."

"Drat," said Louise as the 90s Club trooped out to the lobby. "I thought we'd fingered the murderer."

"Back to the drawing board," grumbled George.

"We don't know she's not the murderer," Nancy said. She took Fitz's arm. "We're going back to our apartment and wait to hear from the sheriff."

"Let us know when he comes so we can be with you," Louise said. "We were perfectly in our rights to hold the gems and jewelry until ownership was established. We've been making every effort to find out who owns them. And also," she concluded triumphantly, "we didn't want to distract the sheriff from his most important task of finding the murderer."

***

That night, the 90s Club sat glumly at Table fifty-six in the dining room, wine glasses full and meals ordered.

"Harmason didn't call," said Nancy.

"Doggone it," said Louise. "I was sure Violet was the murderer."

"None of our suspects has an alibi, and they all had the opportunity," said Fitz. "The motive has got to be wound up with the old trunk and the gemstones. A lot of money there."

Nancy shrugged as she noticed Vicki at another table watching her. Their eyes met, and Vicki walked over.

"How is Bella?" Nancy asked.

"Still in the hospital, but she's much better. How is the investigation going?" she asked. "I've been keeping my ears open but haven't gotten anywhere."

"We're moving along," said Nancy noncommittally. "We appreciate your efforts, though."

Vicki folded her arms and added, "There's a rumor going around that you found a stash of gemstones."

"Where did you hear that?" asked Fitz.

"Some of the ladies were talking." She winked. "They're guessing you've hidden them away." Vicki turned serious. "This better be cleared up soon and the murderer caught, or they might turn on you, accuse you of theft, murder, and who knows what."

"The sheriff will have everything we have as soon as we've listed all the gemstones and cross-referenced them with other lost or stolen items here at Whisperwood. Meanwhile, they're locked away in Harry's safe. They will be returned to the proper owners as soon as possible. This will probably take a week or more," Nancy said stiffly.

"Oh," Vicki bit her lip. "Okay." She waved good-bye and walked back to her table.

"Who's been talking?" asked Louise.

Nancy shook her head. "I know none of us talked. Maybe Harry? He could have told Ashley or Violet or the office manager and they passed it on."

Fitz smiled at Nancy. "I retrieved the video cameras from the basement."

She smiled back and nodded. "Now we need to make sure all of our suspects know where they can find the gems for the next few days. Harry's safe. I already planted the seed with Vicki."

"Uh oh," said George. "That's a dangerous stunt, Nancy, and I disapprove."

Louise looked from one to the other. "What are you talking about?"

"We need you both to help spread the word." Nancy set down her glass hard to show she meant business. "We'll set up the cameras, and maybe we'll trap a murderer this time."

Executive Staff Takes Training Day
Whisperwood's entire executive staff and department supervisors will be at an all-day training retreat next Thursday in the conference facility at The Firestone Inn. Calls will be directed to Ashley at the reception desk who will forward emergency calls to the appropriate personnel and take messages. Thank you for your consideration of this important work.

The Whisperwood Breeze,
Newsletter of Whisperwood
Retirement Village

Chapter 36

Nancy and Fitz walked to Louise's apartment hand in hand, followed by Louise and George. They needed another brainstorming session. They trooped in and took their places in Louise's rickety antique chairs.

"Let's brainstorm motives." Nancy pulled a notebook and pen out of her purse and waited for suggestions.

Fitz began. "News of Glinda's death took time to reach Alex and Sterling and probably others as well. They knew she had a load of gemstones hidden somewhere and figured her prized brassbound trunk was the best bet. That's why they came here—to get their hands on the trunk."

"Barbara and Don Elmo and Glinda's sons, Clark and Cary, didn't know what was hidden in the trunk," Nancy said. "None of them wanted it, so they threw it out and Simon picked it up."

Fitz sat up. The chair creaked. "We agree that Simon must not have known about the gemstones in the trunk or he would have taken it apart himself instead of storing it in the tunnel room."

"He must have started wondering about it, though," Nancy said, "when he heard Alex and Sterling wanted it."

"He might have found the false bottom," added Louise, "and kept it as is, without taking any of the jewelry hidden there out of it for now. After all, he thought he had an impenetrable hiding place."

Fitz stood and paced the room restlessly. "I'll bet he doesn't have any ordinary tools like a screwdriver. Those screws were in tight."

Nancy nodded. "He does have some tools, though," Nancy said thoughtfully," but they are small for working with jewelry."

Nancy finished scribbling in the notebook and looked up. "In summary, Simon picked up the trunk and stowed it away in the tunnel room, but he knew nothing about the gemstones. Alex, Sterling, and Violet Velois came to Whisperwood at about the same time. Alex and Sterling had just received the delayed news of Glinda's death and both knew of the trunk's value. Violet Velois knew Glinda had a stash of gemstones, but nothing more. By coincidence, she was hired as staff here, and her story rings true."

"She's on staff, but she's staying here and taking meals with us," said Louise. "I don't get it."

"I asked Harry about that," Nancy said. "She's waiting for an apartment in town to become available."

George folded his arms and sat back. "Alex Elmo was the victim, and we've decided he was murdered to eliminate a competitor for the trunk. Could there be some other reason? Maybe he was blackmailing someone. Sterling was also murdered, possibly because he may have recognized someone from the past."

"He was also another competitor for the trunk." said Fitz.

"And we think Bella was probably attacked because she stumbled across something that threatened the killer," put in George.

"Alex was a convicted felon," said Louise, picking up her coffee cup "No telling what crimes he might have been mixed up in, but he was Barbara and Don Elmo's grandson. I can't see them killing him or him blackmailing them."

"Glinda's sons, Cary and Clark, haven't been back since they cleared out Glinda's apartment," added Fitz.

"What about Harry?" suggested George.

The others stared at him. "Harry?" said Nancy and turned the idea over in her mind. "No," she said firmly. "Not Harry."

Fitz stopped pacing and sat on the couch, crossing his legs. "Sterling was afraid of being murdered and rightly so. He stayed in his room at the motel and was murdered by someone he didn't expect."

George nodded. "That's true. He would have been my candidate for murderer, but I didn't see him here at Whisperwood. Why was he hanging around?"

"I saw him in town having lunch with the Elmos," Louise said. "He was still hoping to cash in somehow on whatever happened. Anyway, if he was afraid of being murdered, he wouldn't be the killer, would he?"

"Violet Velois, our esteemed life enrichment director, turns out to be LaDianne Richmond, cabaret singer and owner of the lasered diamond we found in Glinda's stash. Somehow Violet seems too cool and in control to be a murderer. She is handsomely paid for her job here and was a successful entertainer unlike Alex and Sterling, who were out-of-luck losers and unemployed."

"But Glinda stole her diamonds," said Louise. "That's why she's here."

"We got to do a better job hiring people," muttered Louise.

George stroked his chin. "I was on the Human Resources Committee that interviewed her. She didn't say anything about being a singer."

"Why would she?" asked Nancy. "That's not the job she applied for. She must have a lot of show business contacts and she has been doing a great job."

Louise glanced around her living room. "The murderer has already searched your apartment, and Malone attacked him or her. What will they do next?"

"I don't think anyone has noticed that we sometimes meet here," Nancy said.

Fitz picked up one of the cameras and placed it next to the television, aiming it at the front hallway. "As they say, a day late and a dollar short, but now anyone entering this apartment will be captured on camera."

"We don't need it here," put in George. "Put it in Nancy's apartment or yours where we've stashed a lot of the stuff we found in the tunnel room."

"What shall we do with the other camera?" asked Louise.

"We're spreading the idea that the gems will be

stored in Harry's office safe when we aren't working on them," said Nancy. "We need to drive the murderer to Harry's office and the safe."

"And a camera," added Fitz.

George snapped his fingers. "Remember that note in *The Whisperwood Breeze*? All the executive staff will be out of the office this Thursday. All day. Perfect opportunity to attack the safe."

Louise grinned. "I see the need for another letter to the residents."

"Good," George said. "Send the murderer to Harry. I don't ever want to be tied up again in fear for my life."

"None of us do," added Fitz. "Maybe this time we can stay out of the murderer's way. Time for the police to take over, I say."

Nancy shrugged. "If they'll listen to us."

Notice to the Residents
Keep Jewelry In A Safe Place

Jewelry and unset gemstones have been found on Whisperwood grounds. If you are missing some piece of jewelry, please contact Harry Doyle with a complete description and your name and contact information.

All residents should store valuable items in their bank, the safe in the Executive Offices, or their apartment's safe located in every apartment's master bedroom closet.

Harry Doyle, Administrator

Chapter 37

The next morning, Nancy arrived early to the lobby to have a quiet talk with Ashley before anyone was around. She explained their plan.

Ashley was thrilled. "You're letting me in on this! I am so excited, and I've got an idea. I always take my coffee breaks at ten a.m. and two p.m. Most people notice when I'm gone, so that will be the perfect time to catch someone breaking in."

Nancy agreed and emailed Fitz. He had set up the camera in Harry's office the afternoon before with Harry's approval.

"I'd like to see the killer caught," Harry had said, "but seems to me he'd be more likely to break in at night."

Fitz nodded as he fiddled with the camera angle. "I would, too, except that a guard is set up in the lobby all night long. He'd see everything going on."

"You're right," Harry conceded, "but then there's Ashley during the day."

"She takes fifteen minutes for coffee breaks morning and afternoon and a lunch break. Everybody here knows her schedule."

"I guess so," Harry said. "And everyone knows the staff will be out of the office today. Good luck then."

After talking with Ashley, Nancy sat at her table in the lobby as planned. She chatted with everyone who walked by, always mentioning that the executive staff were out for the day. Louise and George also roamed the halls, planning casual encounters with Vicki, Barbara, and Don.

Fitz was on an early morning bird hike, but he kept his phone handy and frequently checked the camera images. Nancy waited for him to report if he saw anyone in the office or the apartment. They had no intention of confronting a potential murderer to the relief of all four of them.

"I don't want another broken wrist," Louise said.

"And I'd like to stay out of a car trunk," added Nancy, shivering as she remembered that narrow escape. We've had too many, she thought, and her cherished friends had almost lost their lives several times because of their investigations.

They would send the images to Lt. Harmason and let him reap all the glory while they remained unsung but away from danger.

Fitz returned for lunch and met the other three in the Pub. This time, Ashley joined them. "I told everyone I had to leave early this afternoon. That means no one will be in the office or reception desk all afternoon," she said. "Anything on the camera?"

"Nothing," Fitz reported, "except for Malone. No action in Harry's office either."

"People here are afraid of Malone," Nancy said.

"He could be in danger." He had been poisoned before by criminals at Whisperwood.

"Don't worry." Fitz patted Nancy's hand. "The camera will pick up any funny business."

As they waited for their meals, Nancy's neighbor Caroline happened to pass by and glance in. She waved at them and hurried past.

Nancy waved back, but her mind was on poor Malone. He was not the cuddliest of cats but she loved him and he'd saved her life twice.

"I'm going to run down to my apartment to check on Malone," she said to Fitz. "I'll be right back."

Fitz nodded and pulled out his bird book.

Nancy walked briskly to her apartment, but as she approached, she noticed the door was slightly open. "How did that happen?" she asked herself and walked in, closing it tightly behind her. Malone usually lurked nearby, hoping for a chance to escape, but this time, he was rummaging in the living room and then she heard a kittenish meow as Cleo batted a ball around the floor.

Then she saw Caroline at the desk, opening drawers. "What are you doing?" asked Nancy in complete surprise.

Caroline eyed her as she slid the drawer closed. "Looking for a pen to write you a note," she said. "The door was open and I needed someone to babysit Cleo."

But Nancy knew the door hadn't been open. Caroline had broken in. Suddenly the pieces fell into place. Caroline had moved in around the same time as Sterling and Alex had arrived in town. Caroline's kitty had served to distract all of them, especially Malone. Nancy glanced at the camera, hoping Fitz would look at his phone, but then she saw the camera had been turned off and covered.

If Fitz couldn't get an image, he would know something was wrong and would come, but he might think she had turned it off. After all, they were expecting someone to break into Harry's office, not her apartment. Besides, the perp had had all morning to break into her apartment and search. Why wait until Fitz had returned and Nancy had folded her table? Dinner would be the next logical time for a break-in.

Except Caroline had broken in now.

She saw us at lunch, Nancy thought. "We're always happy to take care of Cleo," she said, backing toward the door.

"Just a minute," Caroline said. "Stop."

Nancy stopped and faced Caroline who now pointed a small revolver at her. "Where are the jewels?"

Nancy held out her hands. "I don't know what you mean."

"All right," Caroline said. "I'll spell it out for you. Glinda's gemstones. I want them. Where are they?" Her eyes narrowed and her mouth was grim. "I mean business." She held up the gun menacingly. "Where are the gemstones?"

"You broke in the other night," said Nancy. "Malone attacked you." Caroline always wore heavy makeup. *That's why I hadn't noticed the cat scratches on her face.*

Caroline's eyes narrowed. "I mistook how mean

that cat is when he's not playing with Cleo. I meant to bring her in to distract him, but she'd hidden somewhere in my apartment, and I needed to be quick."

"I don't have them," Nancy said, one eye on Malone. If only he was up to his usual tricks, but Cleo as usual had him entranced. "They're in Harry's safe."

"Sure. You've been putting the word out, but I don't believe you. Show me your safe."

Buying time, hoping Fitz would show up, she walked slowly into the bedroom to the closet, opened the door, and pushed aside the clothes to reveal the safe.

"Open it," Caroline ordered.

"They aren't in there," Nancy said.

Caroline held the gun as if she would swipe Nancy with it. "Where are they?"

Nancy shrugged. "In Harry's office."

"Don't give me that. Open the safe." Caroline glanced at her watch. "Now."

"All right." Nancy played the elderly card as she groaned to stoop and slowed her movements, holding her back as if it ached. She glanced at the gun. "Is that what you shot Alex and Sterling with?" she asked.

"I'll shoot you, too, if you don't get on with it," Caroline said.

"Why did you kill them? They didn't know where the gems were," said Nancy.

"Too much competition. Anyway, I had to shoot Sterling after he recognized me." She stopped to preen. "I was Glinda's dresser. I handled her wardrobe. She stole from the people she knew, and I stole from her. That's how I got the money to move here."

Nancy slowed down even more. She pretended to study the safe combination lock. Caroline had confessed to the murders. She wouldn't let Nancy escape alive. She hoped Fitz would come to the rescue while Caroline was distracted with the safe, but then he might get hurt. Nancy didn't want him hurt, but what could she do?

This time, Malone was no help. He and Cleo were roughhousing in the kitchen.

Nancy reached for the dial, making her hands shake to buy more time.

"Hands up! Now!"

Nancy raised her hands and turned to see Caroline do the same. In the living room stood Vicki Townsend, gun drawn and pointed at Caroline.

"Drop the gun," Vicki said.

Caroline dropped it and stared open-mouthed at Vicki. "Where did you come from?"

"I've been watching the lot of you," said Vicki. "Knew you were up to something." She looked at Nancy. "Pick up the weapon and take it into the living room, then call 911."

Nancy reached for the gun.

"Now wait a minute," said Caroline. "She has a million dollars in gemstones here in this apartment. How about if we get rid of her and split the take."

"Fifty-fifty?" asked Vicki.

"Sure. Even forty-sixty if you like."

"Thanks, but no thanks. You tried to kill my sister. Call 911, Nancy."

Nancy ran for the phone.

Just then, Fitz opened the door and walked in. He

stared at the tableau in front of him. "What's been going on?" he asked.

Cleaning Up When Clearing Out

If you'll be away from Whisperwood for an extended time, please be sure to take care of all the pesky details to make life easier for other residents and staff.

• Return books to the library.

• Empty trash receptacles and make sure all appliances are off and windows are closed.

• Inform Harry Doyle, Administrator, or Gene Reynolds, Finance Director, so that housekeeping, dining room, and security staff will know of your absence and an accommodation made to your bill.

The Whisperwood Breeze,
Newsletter of Whisperwood
Retirement VIllage

Chapter 38

The police had been and gone, taking Caroline away in handcuffs. Caroline was crying as she left and begging Nancy to take care of Cleo. The 90s Club sat in Nancy's living room, drinking decaf with Vicki.

"I am so grateful to you," said Nancy. "You saved my life and caught the killer, but how did you know...?"

"I'm a retired police investigator," Vicki said with a wink. "Easy for me to pick up on your shenanigans with that secret room in the basement and all the folderol about the missing gemstones, but I had no intention of getting involved. Like I said, I'm retired."

"Why didn't you tell us?" Nancy asked. "We could have used your help."

Vicki laughed. "I liked being one of your suspects and watching you amateurs running around, but then..." She swallowed and cast her eyes down at the floor. Her sadness was palpable. "When Bella was hurt, it got personal, and I didn't know who to trust. Your 90s Club has quite a reputation here, but..."

"Is Bella really your sister?" asked George, frowning at Vicki over his coffee cup.

"Of course she is, and she likes you, George. We

are both retired. We combined our savings and pensions to be able to afford this place."

"We're all very sorry Bella was attacked," said Nancy quietly. The others nodded.

"Thank you," Vicki said. "She's conscious now and improving daily." She set down her cup and rose. "It's been a busy day, and I'm bushed. See you tomorrow."

After she left, Malone and Cleo came out from the kitchen, strolled past the group seated in the living room, and disappeared into the bedroom.

Fitz glanced at Nancy. "I guess we have two cats now?"

Nancy smiled and nodded. "They're inseparable. I wouldn't have the heart to give Cleo away," she said.

Fitz put an arm around her. "Good," he said.

***

The next night at dinner, the 90s Club met again around their favorite table fifty-six.

"Caroline was very clever," said Nancy.

"How so?" asked Louise. "She didn't find the gems and she got caught."

"She must have heard about Malone," said Nancy, "my attack cat and his record of catching crooks."

George arched an eyebrow. "So?"

Nancy glanced at him. "So she brought in Cleo to distract him and distract him she did."

"That means Caroline hid the bug in our apartment," added Fitz. "She knew a lot more about what we were doing than she let on."

Louise tapped on her glass with a spoon. "All right. The case is solved. Now to the important stuff.

Nancy and Fitz, when is the wedding?"

Fitz laughed. "I've got the license. We're ready to roll."

"We've scheduled the chapel for eleven a.m. tomorrow, and Harry got a divinity license online so he can officiate," said Nancy. "Then we booked the private dining room for lunch to celebrate."

"Great!" said Louise and George together. "And where are we going for the honeymoon?"

"We'll see," said Fitz, smiling at Nancy.

Wedding Announcement

Nancy Dickenson and Fitzhugh Connelly are pleased to announce their marriage in the Whisperwood Chapel on Saturday. Whisperwood Administrator Harry Doyle officiated and Louise Owens and George Burroughs witnessed the ceremony. The bride wore an elegant tealength, French blue dress with chiffon lace. They plan a honeymoon cruise in the British Isles accompanied by Louise and George. Congratulations and best wishes to Nancy and Fitz!

The Whisperwood Breeze,
Newsletter of Whisperwood
Retirement Village

THE END

All of the 90s Club books are available as paperbacks and e-books.

If you enjoyed this book, please post a review on Amazon.com, Goodreads, and other websites.

Eileen loves hearing from her readers. Visit her website at SecretPanels.net and e-mail her at eileenmcintire2017@gmail.com.

www.ingramcontent.com/pod-product-compliance
Lightning Source LLC
Chambersburg PA
CBHW051140190726
48290CB00006B/1933